# CODY'S RIDE

# CODY'S RIDE

## Stan Wiseman

Walker and Company
New York

First published in the United States of America in 1993
by Walker Publishing Company, Inc.

Published simultaneously in Canada by Thomas Allen & Son
Canada, Limited, Markham, Ontario.

Library of Congress Cataloging-in-Publication Data
Wiseman, Stan.
Cody's ride / Stan Wiseman.
p.   cm.
ISBN 0-8027-1266-5
I. Title.
PS3573.I8445C63   1993
813'.54—dc20      92-35804
CIP

Printed in the United States of America

2   4   6   8   10   9   7   5   3   1

# CODY'S RIDE

# CHAPTER 1

CODY Bailey slouched in a scarred and battered ladderback chair in Silas Bonner's stuffy office, absentmindedly flicking the rowel of his spur. As the early morning sun filtered through the grimy pane of the room's only window, Cody glanced at Silas standing beside the big rolltop desk.

"Somebody's got to make that ride, Silas," Cody said. "And this is my route. Why shouldn't I go?"

Silas scratched his scalp through his thinning white hair. The seams in his leathery face deepened into furrows as he grimaced.

"It ain't just you, Bailey," he said, his voice grating like gravel under a wagon wheel. "I don't want nobody makin' that run. Them Injuns don't care about the mail. You could wear a sign on yer back sayin' 'Pony Express' and it wouldn't stop them from attackin'. Probably be like waving a red flag in front of a bull. And you know it."

Cody crossed his arms in disgust. He resented his boss's doubts, even though he liked Silas. The station manager was the closest thing Cody had to kin in these parts. His folks had taught him to respect his elders and he didn't care to argue with the old man. Still, it was his job to deliver the mail and he aimed to see it done, Indians or no Indians.

"Have you got any orders from St. Joe to stop the mail?"

Silas hooked his gnarled, arthritic thumbs in his suspenders as he gazed at Cody. He showed no favoritism among his men, but he held Cody in high esteem. The

1

young man took his job seriously, willingly taking on tasks many other riders considered beneath their dignity.

"No, I ain't heard from St. Joe," he grumbled.

"Well, then," Cody said as he unfolded his lean five-foot-eight-inch frame and stood. "When that mochila comes in day after tomorrow I'm throwing it over my saddle and headin' west."

He started for the door.

"Suit yerself, Bailey," Silas growled. "But when yer scalp ends up hangin' from some Injun's lance, you remember I tried to tell ya."

Cody turned to the old man, a smile parting his thin lips and mischief dancing in his blue eyes. "Don't reckon I'll be in much shape to remember anything if it comes to that." He pushed the door open and walked out.

Twenty-year-old Cody strolled briskly across the dusty station yard to the stable. He had ridden with the Pony Express since its inception the previous year. His first route had covered the road from St. Joe to Kinnekuk. He hadn't missed a ride and didn't intend to start now.

The rusty hinges on the stable door squawked as the door swung open. Cody strode to the stall where his favorite mount, a gelding named Champion, stood with his head raised as Cody approached.

Cody threw his saddle on the black and white mustang, a horse as lean and wiry as himself. He hooked the near side stirrup over the saddle horn, then reached beneath the horse and grabbed the latigo. He fed the leather through the cinch ring. Cody pulled the cinch too tight, causing Champion to nicker in protest.

"Sorry, Champ," he said, loosening the girth. He patted the mustang's neck, wondering if Silas had lost confidence in his ability to get the mail through. "Guess I'm just outa sorts a bit."

He led Champion out of the stable and into the yard, shooting an angry glance toward the weatherbeaten house that served as the headquarters of the Pony station and the relay for the Overland Stage. He didn't understand Silas Bonner's attitude. Cody had been the station keeper's only rider for months, and thanks to him, Silas had one of the best records in Slade's Division, which extended from Fort Kearny in the east to Horseshoe Station in Wyoming Territory. Silas had never demonstrated anything but firm determination when it came to getting the mail through, until this morning. That puzzled Cody.

"How about a trip to town, boy?" Cody said as he climbed into the saddle. "I hope Jim Wilkes has got them new Colts in. Way Silas talks we might be needin' 'em."

Once astride Champion, Cody gently spurred the mustang to an easy lope. They headed toward Parker's Junction, a bustling settlement along the river, a mile and a half northwest of the Pony station. The town consisted of a few houses, blacksmith shop, general store, and a couple of saloons that also rented rooms. Cody reckoned he would find the town more crowded than usual, what with all the rumors about Indian attacks. When such stories started circulating, the men who ran the small ranches in the surrounding prairie usually poured into the Junction to stock up on staples and ammunition. The influx only lasted a short time, as the ranchers could ill afford an extended absence from their homes.

Cody thought all the excitement was a waste. No news had come verifying an Indian attack anywhere near the Junction, though a few sightings had occurred along the trail and there really wasn't anything unusual about that. Cody had come to the conclusion that most folks became downright jumpy when it came to Indians. He figured everyone around these parts knew most of the Indian trouble was still out west. The Piutes continued making mischief along the Chorpenning line, as the Central Route west of Salt Lake was called, but they hadn't shut it down as they had the year before. Of course some of the Sioux and Cheyenne stole horses from time to time and that led to violence now and again, but for the most part, conflict had been limited.

Only a few months ago he had met a Sioux brave on the plains. He had approached the Indian cautiously, while trying to show he intended him no harm. Using wide gestures, the brave related how he came to be afoot. Cody rightly interpreted from the sign language that the Indian's horse had somehow broken its leg, leaving its rider stranded on the prairie. He patted Champion's rump, then extended his hand, offering this new acquaintance a ride. At first the Indian had exhibited some reluctance, and Bailey hadn't blamed him for that. If the situation had been reversed he wouldn't have been eager to mount. But the young brave hopped up behind him.

Upon the unlikely pair's arrival at the Sioux encampment, Cody received a more formal introduction by a craggy-faced old man, Red Eagle, who spoke fractured, but understandable, English. He told Cody the young brave was named Standing Bear. Bailey had liked the old man and Standing Bear, who vowed to return Cody's kindness one day. The other Indians, however, watched him carefully and, he thought, with a great deal of suspicion. He imagined that the people in Parker's Junction would probably have reacted the same way if he had ridden into town behind a redskin. He was struck deeply by how similar each group was in its wariness of the other.

The ride to Parker's Junction passed quickly. It seemed to Cody that whenever he rode Champion the ride always ended too soon. The horse was bridle-wise and responsive to the slightest of Cody's movements. Second only to the exhilaration of running Champion flat out, he enjoyed the horse's smooth, loping gait. He rocked gently in the saddle, letting Champion carry him like a tumbleweed on the breeze.

He admired the rolling prairie, as wide and open as the

clear sky overhead. Most people who passed through derisively referred to this vast wilderness as a desert. Cody, however, had come to love this land, making many treks over it while hauling freight for Russell, Majors & Waddell. About a year earlier, when word had gone out that the freighters intended to establish the first fast mail line across the continent, Cody had made it known he wanted to ride.

He reined Champion to a walk as they entered the Junction. Dust hung in the air, stirred up by all the hubbub in the Junction's main street. Not only were the locals bustling around, but Cody noticed a small emigrant train had pulled into town, apparently to stock up at Wilkes's General Store before proceeding into the barren wilderness that awaited them. The emigrants' children scampered over and under the prairie schooners, laughing and hollering, oblivious to the hazards that lay ahead.

As he rode past Hanzel's Livery, Cody saw another contributor to the swirling clouds of dust. A big sorrel in the German blacksmith's pole corral was fighting Hanzel and his two sons. The men had one rope around the beast's neck, trying to drag him to a snubbing post. Cody rode to the edge of the corral and dismounted. He climbed onto the top bar and sat down to watch as the Hanzels finally brought the horse to the post.

"Whew!" Cody hollered, waving the dust away from his face with his wide-brimmed hat. "You fellars are stirrin' up more dust than a prairie twister."

The blacksmith pulled a soiled handkerchief from his back pocket to wipe the sweat from his forehead, only succeeding in smearing the dirt and filling the deep lines in his face with a black crust.

"Mebbe you climb don here und help shoe dis devil, Bailey. We 'bout ready to trow him don und stake him out."

Cody held up his hands. "Sorry, Herman, but I've got a

ride comin' up pretty soon, and I sure couldn't make it if I let that ornery critter there throw me around your corral."

The big man nodded and smiled. "Yup, he bust you up, dat's for shore."

"Is it all right if I leave Champ tied up here? I've got some business down the street with Wilkes."

"Shore, shore. Just tie him by de trough."

"Thanks, Herman."

Cody swung his legs over the corral bar and dropped to the ground. He led Champion to the hitch rail by the water trough and tied him there. The mustang lowered his head to the water and began to drink as he shifted his forelegs. Cody gave the horse an affectionate pat on the rump as he walked behind him, heading for Wilkes's. The clamor of shouting men and the shrieking sorrel erupted from the corral as he sauntered toward the general store.

He stepped onto the wide porch of Wilkes's store and peered through the doorway. The storekeeper and his wife were busy fetching this box of ammunition, that bag of flour, or this axe handle for the demanding customers wedged in front of the counter. Mrs. Wilkes's hair, usually pulled tight in a bun at the back of her head, waved in loose strands like willow limbs. In less than a minute Cody heard Mr. Wilkes say, "If everybody will just be patient, we'll get to you as fast as we can" at least three times. Cody pushed back his hat on his head, watching the commotion with wonder. He decided it would be just as foolish, if not as dangerous, to wade through this crowd as it would have been to jump into Hanzel's corral.

Looking over his shoulder at the chaos in the store, he stepped off the porch and bumped into the broad chest of a hulking man with hard gray eyes and the flexibility of stone.

"Pardon me, mister," Cody apologized.

"Ya need to watch where yer goin', runt," the big man

growled hatefully. Placing a beefy hand on Cody's shoulder he gave the Pony rider a rough shove that nearly sent him sprawling. "Get in my way again and I'll break ya in half."

His cheeks burning with anger and embarrassment, Cody walked down the street to Everson's Saloon & Restaurant without so much as a glance behind him.

A slate on an easel stood by the saloon's entrance, touting the meal of the day as venison stew with "genuwine gardin vegtables and freshbaked bread." Cody stood in the doorway, giving his eyes time to adjust to the dim light within the saloon.

"Come for drinkin' or eatin', Bailey?" Bob Everson called from the sober side of the bar.

Cody's spurs sang as he ambled up to the bar, which consisted of two twelve-foot planks laid across three whiskey barrels. After emptying them of their fiery contents, Everson had loaded them half full of dirt to provide the bar with stability. He had built his saloon of cedar logs and it stood thirty feet long and nearly forty feet deep. A few crude tables and chairs were strewn haphazardly over the wooden floor. A loft above the saloon had served as the owner's home until recently, when Everson had moved into his new house on the edge of town. Now he had beds for rent in the loft.

"You know I took the company oath against drinkin', Bob," Cody said as he grasped the weathered crown of his hat and dropped it onto the bar.

"Venison stew it is, then." He turned toward a low doorway directly behind the bar that led into the kitchen. "Harley! The Pony rider wants some stew!"

Everson's cook, a reed-thin, hawk-nosed old man poked his head through the doorway. "Is that you, Cody?"

"It's me, Harley. How about makin' sure you get some of that deer meat on my plate?"

Harley cackled. "Boy, don' choo worry none 'bout that. Yep, you have . . ."

Bailey didn't hear the rest, as the old man had drawn his head back into the kitchen while mumbling.

"Ever see so many people in the Junction?" Everson asked.

"Can't say as I have," Cody responded. "Folks sure are makin' a fuss over a bunch of rumors."

"Been to Wilkes's?"

"Hmmph! Didn't bring a crowbar to help me get in the door."

"Yeah, he's got quite a crowd over there. I think the price of flour's dern near tripled in the last hour."

"Seen a fella over there, big man, moved like a buffalo. Wide face. You know him?"

"Can't say as I do. Why?"

"No reason, I guess."

Harley brought Cody his stew, scooting the bent and dented tin plate over the bar top. Cody fished his fork out of the thick, greasy gravy. He stuck the handle of the utensil in his mouth, licking it, then shifted it to his left hand while he lapped the gravy from his thumb and forefinger.

"Seems you forgot somethin' here, Bob," Cody said.

"How's that?"

"Sign out front said fresh bread with your stew."

"Ah, that Harley. Sometimes I think his brain ain't in town."

Everson ducked through the low doorway behind the bar. A moment later he returned with a slice of bread and dropped it on Cody's plate.

"Why, this bread ain't fresh," Cody said after he took his first bite.

Everson smiled.

"Was yesterday."

Cody shook his head. He picked up his plate and started for one of the rough-hewn tables scattered about the floor.

"Bailey! You cussed whelp! I knowed that was you!"

Cody recognized the voice immediately.

"Pop McCready!" Cody set his plate down on the table where a stout man with an unkempt beard hanging to his chest sat smiling at him.

"Pull up a chair, boy," Pop said in his deep rolling voice.

Cody plopped into a chair across the table. "Last I heard you were still workin' the jerk line to Santa Fe," he said around a mouthful of stew.

"Naw! I give that up. I'm figgerin' on doin' me some pannin' out in the Jefferson Territory."

"I expect all the good claims are gone."

"Reckon I'll find 'nough gold to tend to my needs."

"I hope you ain't travelin' alone. There's been a lot of talk about Indian trouble."

McCready's washed-out green eyes narrowed. "Yeah, I been hearin' 'bout yer Injun trouble. Let me tell you, I got an idee they's more to it. Sometimes folks is a mite too quick to be blamin' ever'thin' on Injuns."

Cody laid his fork on the edge of his plate, staring across the table at the old skinner.

# CHAPTER 2

JOSEPH "Big Joe" Murphy stared at the emigrant men through humorless steel-gray eyes set too close together in a wide face. The jabbering of the pilgrims, coupled with the racket raised by their brats, had begun to irritate the pilot of the emigrant train. He scratched his jaw through a bushy black beard dusted with flecks of gray. A dark tobacco stain below his thick mustache gave the only sign that a mouth existed within the dense brush covering the lower half of his face. He towered over the former store-keepers and farmers, an immense man with huge biceps and a broad chest that strained against the rawhide stitching of his sweat-stained buckskin shirt. He wore a medallion the size of a silver dollar on a thin strip of leather around his neck. It was his good luck charm, taken from a Mexican officer at the Battle of San Jacinto many years before. He had worn it ever since, never removing it for any reason. It was an odd attachment for a man who scoffed at the superstitions of others.

His intimidating demeanor had kept the men from approaching him before now with their concerns. But with their arrival in Parker's Junction and the visible apprehension of the locals regarding Indian activities, they knew they could no longer keep silent.

The emigrant train consisted of five families. There were the Ruthefords, Carl, his wife, Mary, and their daughter, Jenny; the Bakers and their four boys; the Franklins, with two daughters and a son; the Jeffersons and their two sons; and the Carters, with four sons and two daughters. Eleven of the children in the train were

10

over fifteen years old. While the older children had gone to help tote supplies from Wilkes's store, seventeen-year-old Jenny kept an eye on the younger children.

Through no desire or campaign of his own, Carl Rutheford had become the leader and spokesman for the emigrants. However, when he had approached Murphy, the others had gone along. Now everyone talked at once, and Carl could see Murphy's fuse smoldering. They had hired Murphy as the result of a unanimous vote after meeting him in Independence. But ever since their departure, the pilot had been rude to the women and surly toward the children. He had brusquely dismissed any input from the men, reminding them at every opportunity that they were only pilgrims. Over the last few weeks he had grown insufferable. Carl Rutheford and Jacob Carter had even tried to find another guide at Fort Kearny, but to no avail. And now this talk of Indian trouble threatened to rupture the train.

Suddenly Murphy had had enough. "Now, y'all listen to me!"

Everyone instantly fell silent. Even the children, previously unaware of the confrontation between their fathers and the pilot, froze in the midst of their play, the dust settling about them.

"I've had about enough of yer bellyachin'!"

"Please, Mr. Murphy," Carl began hesitantly. "We're only suggesting we wait here until we can connect with another train. That would provide more protection for all of us."

"Don't you tenderfoots understand? We ain't got no time to be waitin' for late starters. Any folks follerin' us ain't gonna find one blade of grass along the trail for their stock, and that's gonna slow 'em down. If ya want time to get yer new homes built before winter we got to keep movin'."

He snapped the floppy-brimmed brown hat off his head

and slapped it against his leg, causing a cloud of dust to explode from its battered crown.

"Well, sir, I ain't gonna have no part of it!" Murphy bellowed. "Y'all just sit here and wait if that's what ya want. But I'm 'spectin' payment for my services."

The pilot's cold eyes, filled with contempt, swept over the pale faces staring openmouthed at him. He knew they had tried to replace him at Fort Kearny. He didn't care.

"Come mornin'," he growled, "I'll be headin' west. Y'all can do what ya want. Right now I see a saloon, and I sure can use a drink."

He pushed roughly through the men and strode across the street to Everson's.

Jenny Rutheford's blue eyes followed the hulking pilot as he stepped through the doorway into Everson's Saloon. She had heard her father and mother talking about him the last few nights. They hadn't asked her opinion, but if they had, she would have told them she didn't like him one bit. On more than one occasion she had caught him leering at her, and it had made her skin crawl. An involuntary shiver ran up her spine as she watched Murphy disappear into the saloon. Her eyes fell on the men huddled together where the pilot had left them. The men had to decide what must be done. She returned to watching the children, wishing for the hundredth time they had stayed in Ohio.

Cody was about to ask Pop McCready just what he had meant about people being quick to blame the Indians for the current unrest when Joe Murphy's massive bulk filled the doorway. McCready looked away from Cody and at the man entering Everson's establishment. Cody followed his gaze, watching as the big man stepped up to the bar.

"You know him?" Cody asked, recognizing the stranger as the man he had bumped into outside Wilkes's store.

"Yep. Name's Murphy," McCready said quietly as he

nodded. "Last time I seen him was down Texas way some years ago. He was a Comanchero then."

Cody frowned. "Seems like I've heard of them before."

"Mean bunch, boy. They traded with the Comanches, sometimes helped get white captives back to their folks. Other times—" The old skinner shrugged.

Cody turned back in his chair. "What d'ya reckon he's doin' here, Pop?"

"I dunno," he replied, his eyes still fixed on Murphy.

Cody dismissed the man at the bar from his thoughts. He had seen all of the man he cared to. Besides, he wanted to hear McCready's theory about the Indian trouble.

"What did you mean when you said some folks was too quick to blame the Indians for everything?"

Pop McCready was reluctant to let the pilot out of his sight, but Cody pressed him for an answer.

"Well, Cody, it strikes me mighty peculiar there ain't been no real fightin', just a load a gab. Kinda gets me to thinkin' somebody's tryin' to get folks all worked up 'bout the Injuns attackin'."

Cody shook his head. "I don't get you, Pop."

Neither of them noticed that Joe Murphy had taken an interest in their conversation while he held a glass of whiskey to his lips. As he listened to McCready and Bailey talking, he sent the whiskey down his throat, then set the glass down on the bar. He motioned for Everson to fill it again. The bartender refilled the glass.

"Leave the bottle, barkeep," Murphy ordered gruffly.

Everson set it down and turned away.

"What I'm tellin' ya," McCready said, "is I ain't so sure all these sightins we been hearin' 'bout are the real McCoy. Injuns don't usually get slicked up for war and go 'round showin' themselves unless they're on the prod and ready to take scalps."

"If folks aren't really seein' Indians, then what are they

seein'?" Cody asked as he scooped a forkful of stew from his plate.

"Mebbe somebody playin' Injun."

McCready leaned across the table and stared hard into Cody's eyes; then, with an almost imperceptible movement of his head, he nodded toward the bar. Cody started to turn, but Pop stopped him.

"Don't."

"Him?" Cody whispered. "What makes you think that?"

McCready sat back in his chair.

"Oh, I dunno. Some trouble I heard 'bout down in Texas a few years back."

Cody wolfed down the rest of the greasy stew, mopping up the last of the gravy with Everson's day-old bread. He didn't know whether to believe Pop or not. But he knew the old man had a sixth sense when it came to Indians. When they had worked together, hauling freight for Russell, Majors & Waddell, McCready's knack for smelling out Indians had saved their lives more than once.

"Well," Cody said, his cheek bulging with the last of his lunch. "Whether there are Indians or not, I got a brace of pistols waitin' for me over at Wilkes's store that'll come in right handy, I expect."

"I take it yer still ridin' the Pony?"

"That's a fact. Got a ride comin' up in a couple days."

McCready stroked his scraggly beard.

"I'd be watchin' my topknot if'n I's you, Bailey."

"You bet. And you keep an eye out for claim jumpers when you land in Jefferson Territory."

"That I will, boy. That I will."

Cody's chair scraped the floor as he pushed back from the table. He pulled the broad-brimmed hat down over the tight black ringlets that covered his head.

"You ought to come by the station before you head west, if you get a chance," he told Pop, who nodded.

Cody started for the door. He shot a swift glance at the

big bear of a man hunched over the bar. He rubbed his chin, thinking about what McCready had said, then walked out. Two steps outside the door he stopped, squinting in the bright afternoon sunshine. The town had quieted down some since his arrival. His eyes fell on the emigrant train at the end of the street and he noticed right away that the children had ceased playing. He was sure that had contributed greatly to the present calm. As he turned toward Wilkes's store a movement near the wagons caught his eye.

Suddenly he saw Jenny Rutheford. He froze in midstep. He had never seen anyone like her. Her blue gingham bonnet had fallen from its perch, hanging tenuously by the slender strings tied at her throat. Strands of yellow hair escaped the thick braid that lay across her right shoulder. Cody couldn't remember when he had seen skin so white and soft looking. The girl's wide blue eyes glistened like sunlight on the surface of a placid stream. Cody choked. He realized those luminous eyes had turned on him. He resisted the impulse to run, but hadn't yet worked up the courage needed to cross the street and introduce himself. He knew he must appear foolish to her, just standing there staring. He swallowed hard and headed toward the train. He looked both ways as he crossed the street, then down at his boots, certain he would see lead weights on them. As he tried to simmer down he noticed she hadn't taken her eyes off him. His mouth went dry.

Cody had just begun to regain some of his natural aplomb when he realized he didn't know what he would say to her. And now the girl stood only a few steps in front of him. He removed his hat as he cleared his throat.

"Howdy, miss."

She smiled easily, warmly.

"Hello."

Cody feared melting into the dust like butter in the hot sun.

"My name's Bailey. Cody Bailey," he said as he extended his hand. A shock jolted through his body as he grasped her hand.

"Pleased to meet you, Mr. Bailey. My name is Jenny Rutheford."

Her voice had a soothing quality, like the sound of rippling water on a hot summer day.

"The pleasure's mine, Miss Rutheford."

"You can call me Jenny, if you'd like. And may I call you Cody?"

He nodded.

"Good. I was just about to walk over to that store," she said, pointing at Wilkes's. "Everyone else went earlier and my mother told me they had some material I might like."

Cody grinned at his good fortune. "So happens I got business there myself. Mind if I walk along with you?"

"Thank you. I'd like that."

They started up the street, neither one in a hurry to reach their destination.

"Where're you from, Jenny?"

"Ohio."

"Everybody in the train from there?"

She nodded. "Everyone except for Mr. Murphy, our pilot. I don't know where he's from."

"Murphy? You mean that fella big as an ox that's over at Everson's?"

"Everson's?"

"That saloon yonder," he said, pointing back in the direction they had come.

"Yes, he was in there. You were too, weren't you?"

"Yeah, but not for liquor. I had lunch over there while I was waitin' for the crowd to thin out at Wilkes's."

"You don't drink alcohol, then?"

"No, miss, I don't. I took the oath."

"The oath?"

"That's right. I ride the Pony and I pledged I wouldn't

touch no liquor, or do no swearin', but that I'd do everything I could to see that the mail goes through."

She stopped and looked at him, her full lips parted in a wide smile. "You ride for the Pony Express?"

"Well, yeah."

"Oh, I've read about you. I mean, all of you riders. It sounds like such an exciting life. If I'd been born a boy, I'd ride with you."

"I'm sure glad you weren't."

He reddened as the words left his mouth, but Jenny only smiled. "Where are y'all headed?" he asked.

"Oh, Pa wants to settle in Denver where his brother lives. He had a good business back in Cincinnati, but I guess he just got tired of it."

Cody thought he detected a note of irritation creeping into her voice. He decided to change the subject. "Are you goin' to be in Parker's Junction long?"

She shook her head. "Just until tomorrow morning, I think. I heard the men talking to Mr. Murphy earlier. They were worried about all this Indian talk and they wanted to stay here and join a larger train, but I guess Mr. Murphy has talked them out of that."

Cody didn't make any attempt to hide his disappointment. She had her journey ahead of her, and he had his ride. Still, he wished they could have had a little more time to get acquainted.

# CHAPTER 3

MURPHY corked the whiskey bottle and grabbed its neck. He didn't like the conversation he had overheard. He spun away from the bar and strode outside. He saw Cody and Jenny strolling up the street toward the general store. He was feeling the rotgut; the liquor stoked the fires of his lust for the young Rutheford girl.

His eyes narrowed as he watched the two young people disappear through the doorway of the store. He wanted to go after them, but he had other business to take care of. The conversation he had overheard between that kid and the mule skinner in the saloon had disturbed him. He had heard the kid tell the skinner he had a run in a couple of days for the Pony Express, so Murphy didn't expect to see the kid again. However, the old man bothered him. The skinner looked familiar, but Murphy couldn't place him. Perhaps he worked for the army.

The pilot ran his finger under his nose and sniffed. He wasn't about to let anyone louse up his plans. He pulled the cork from the whiskey bottle with his teeth and spat it into the dust. He brought the bottle to his lips and tipped his head back. He drained its contents in three long gulps, then pitched it into the street. A deep rumble drew his attention to the darkening sky in the southwest. Rain was coming.

He dragged his heavy boots through the powdery dirt that blanketed the street, but the rising breeze quickly swept away the dust clouds kicked up by Murphy's well-worn boot heels. He shuffled around the train and, to his

18

surprise, found that the emigrants had spotted the rising storm clouds and had begun securing the animals.

Murphy noticed a bench on the wide porch of the general store. It looked to be a likely spot to sit for a spell. Besides, from there he could keep an eye on that girl and the entrance to Everson's Saloon. He smiled as he started toward Wilkes's, his boots scuffing along the street. He congratulated himself on finding a way to stick to business while tending to some pleasure as well.

Mr. Wilkes had started his store in a long, narrow soddy, but last year, just before the Pony Express had started running, he had built this new, larger building. The storefront faced south and had broad windows on either side of the double doors that opened onto the porch. Shelves lined the long walls, and several tables, arranged with narrow aisles between them, stood end to end on the floor. Wilkes had divided his store into two sales areas. When a person came through the entrance he found building supplies, stoves, well pulleys, and tools, along with stable and horse supplies, to his right. The other half of the store contained food items and housekeeping goods, as well as soft goods: blankets, bolts of brightly colored cloth and notions. Centered along the back wall was an eight foot counter with a polished mahogany top. Beneath this, Wilkes had installed a small safe. Behind the counter a black curtain covered the doorway leading into the storeroom. Wilkes emerged through that doorway.

"Here you are, Cody," he said as he placed a package wrapped in brown paper on top of the counter.

Cody studied it for a brief moment, then stripped the paper away, exposing a plain wooden box. He removed the lid. He whistled softly and shook his head.

"They're awful pretty," he said, admiring the walnut handled revolvers. He reached into the box, drawing one of the pistols out. Cradling it in the palm of his hand, he closed his fingers around the cool steel.

"I see you didn't wear your old Remington."

"Only got so much room in my sash. And I plan on wearin' these home."

"Well, I'll tell you what, Cody," Wilkes said, reaching beneath the counter. "The first load is on me."

The storekeeper produced a small crate containing a powder flask, molded balls, and a bag of caps, and set it on the shiny mahogany counter.

"Why, thank you, Mr. Wilkes," Cody said. As he began measuring out the black powder his eyes gleamed like a kid's on Christmas morning.

"If I'm not mistaken, the extra cylinders you ordered are underneath all of that wadding in the box. I got to tell you, I'm a mite curious why you're totin' so much hardware. I thought you Pony riders prided yourselves on ridin' light?"

Cody shrugged as he began ramming the balls into the chambers. "I always had me a hankerin' to carry two guns. Don't really know why, just have."

He snapped the rammer into place, then released the hammer. Cody didn't own a holster, but carried his weapons in a red sash he wore about his waist. Taking the handle of the newly loaded Colt in his right hand, he shoved the revolver into the sash beneath his left rib cage, butt forward. He loaded the second pistol, then placed it in his sash, opposite the first gun.

"Fine looking pair of handguns," Wilkes said.

Cody turned from the counter to show off his new weapons. Instead he saw Joe Murphy step onto the porch. He watched the pilot cup his hands around his eyes as he pressed his face against the window. The blood rushed into Cody's face as he saw Murphy's bloodshot eyes search out Jenny. The drunken guide turned his eyes on the Pony rider. Cody glared at him. Murphy sneered before turning away and noisily depositing his massive bulk onto the bench in front of the store.

The racket drew everyone's attention to the porch, except for Cody's; his gaze fell upon Jenny. A sickly pallor stole the color from her cheeks and he saw anxiety in her eyes. He reckoned she feared Murphy, and he had his suspicions why. Cody decided to allay her fear. He plucked the spare cylinders from the box and tucked them into his sash. He crossed the room to where Jenny and Mrs. Wilkes stood staring at Murphy's broad back.

"You let me know when you're ready to leave, Jenny," he said. "And I'll walk you back to your wagon."

She looked up at his deeply tanned face, her eyes filled with relief. "I would be grateful, Cody."

Mrs. Wilkes smiled at him.

The sky suddenly turned slate gray as the storm from the southwest rolled into Parker's Junction. The light breeze that had blown most of the day became a gale that carried the fine prairie dust aloft, raking everything in its path. Cody heard the wind-driven grains snapping against the windows. He had hoped the stinging wind would drive Murphy from his post, but the brutish man merely pulled his hat down low over his bushy brow.

Though he had no desire for a confrontation with the pilot, Bailey knew he had to get Jenny back to her people before the sky opened up. Now he wished he had worn his old Remington pistol today. He had practiced diligently with that old gun and had become quite adept at drawing it quickly from his sash and hitting what he aimed at. Cody had no doubts about the quality of the sidearms he had just received, but the thought of relying on unfamiliar weapons made him uneasy. Nevertheless, the way he saw it, he had no choice. He had promised the girl his protection.

"Jenny, looks like there's a powerful storm blowin' up. I reckon we best get you back to your folks."

She forced a smile. "Are you sure, Cody?"

"She can stay here till the storm breaks," Jim Wilkes offered.

"Don't know when that might be, Mr. Wilkes. Besides, I gotta be gettin' back to the station, and I promised Jenny I'd see her back to the train."

The storekeeper nodded.

Cody adjusted the Colts in his sash.

Murphy had pulled his hat down against the stinging dust, determined to keep his seat until the girl came out. He didn't intend to let that Pony rider get in his way, either. He figured he could brush the kid aside with less effort than it took to swat a fly. He had started to imagine having the Rutheford girl all to himself, when he saw Pop McCready come through the doorway of Everson's. His gray eyes narrowed as he peered from beneath the brim of his hat at McCready. He watched the skinner untie a horse and pack mule from the rail in front of the saloon and start around to the back of the building. The pilot swore under his breath. Business and pleasure had just taken diverging paths. The emigrant girl had to wait, but there would be plenty of time for her later. He had to deal with McCready now.

Without a glance at the store behind him, Murphy drew up to his full six-foot-four-inch height and propelled himself off the porch. Setting his face into the gusty wind, he headed for Everson's. As Murphy reached the corner around which McCready had disappeared, the sky opened up with a torrential downpour. The pilot cursed himself for not thinking to get his oilskin when he had first seen the storm coming up. In seconds the rain had soaked his clothes. A rivulet ran off the brim of his hat in front of his face; he felt another cascading down his back. The discomfort only added to his already ugly mood.

Behind the saloon Murphy discovered a stable built into the side of a hill. The front and parts of the sides were constructed of cedar logs. The rest of the building was sod. The lone door at the stable entrance stood ajar. Murphy wrapped his beefy fingers around the butt of the heavy Walker Colt in the holster he wore high on his left hip. He crept closer to the stable, his hard eyes fixed on the doorway. When he reached the crude structure he flattened himself against the facade and began edging his way toward the entrance. Suddenly he stopped. In the pouring rain he couldn't be sure, but he thought he heard voices inside. More carefully than before, he started moving along the front of the building. He reached the door, straining to discern the words emanating from the darkened depths of the dugout.

". . . at first I warn't shore, but when I seen that Murphy here I knew that was it. He was accused o' pullin' the same shenanigans down in Texas."

"We've got to be positive. I can't ride back to Fort Laramie and present the colonel with a bunch of assumptions. I need some kind of proof."

The pilot cautiously peeked around the edge of the opening. McCready had his back to the door, resting his elbow on the mule's rump. A much younger man, with sandy hair and sporting a handlebar mustache, faced the old teamster. The young man held a black slicker, of the type issued to the cavalry, folded over his left arm, though he wore no uniform. Murphy studied his face, but didn't recall seeing him anywhere in the settlement before now.

"Looky here, Cap'n," Pop protested. "Them folks gonna pay with their lives to git ya that kind of proof."

"I don't like it any better than you, but my hands are tied."

Murphy slunk away from the entrance and took refuge under a narrow overhang at the corner of the stable. The roof did little to protect him from the drenching rain, but he hadn't sought this position for shelter from the storm. He kept the door in sight until the man with the black slicker emerged from the stable. Murphy stepped back from the front of the building, out of the man's line of vision. A moment later the black slicker swished by, the head of its wearer bowed against the rain.

With long strides, Murphy bounded to the stable entrance, pulling the heavy Colt from its holster. He halted at the door, then peered inside. Pop McCready stood with his back to Murphy, stripping the cumbersome parcels from the pack mule. Murphy burst through the door with surprising quickness for a man of his bulk. Pop turned toward the crash, but Murphy was on him like a bobcat as he came around and landed a crushing blow with his revolver across the bridge of the mule skinner's nose.

Blood exploded from the gash on McCready's face. He staggered backward, stumbling over one of the canvas-covered packs on the stable floor. As he fell he rolled to his left, jerking his Beal's Army .44 from his waistband. He came unsteadily to his feet, blinking his eyes rapidly, trying to clear them of stinging tears. McCready raised his right arm, aiming his pistol at the formless mass towering over him. The thick, calloused fingers of Murphy's left hand snapped closed like the jaws of a bear trap around Pop's right wrist and pushed downward until the .44 fell from the skinner's hand. Murphy struck Pop above the left ear with the Walker. The old man's legs buckled beneath the blow. The pilot took hold of McCready's shirt front as he commenced clubbing him with his gun. Only Murphy's hold kept McCready on his feet as one hammer blow after another rained down on his head. Blood poured from several wounds, and Pop's jaw had gone slack. The savage bludgeoning finally ceased when Murphy, gasping for breath, released his hold on the skinner's shirt. Pop collapsed in a bloody heap on the cold, hard floor. Murphy stood over him, his eyes glassy as his broad chest heaved, threatening the seams of his buckskin shirt, sweat dripping from the end of his nose. He knew the skinner was dead.

After a few moments his breathing settled down. He surveyed the stable to make sure he didn't leave any sign of his presence there. Satisfied that no evidence remained, he moved toward the door. He halted briefly, gazing into the driving rain. He didn't expect to see anyone. A sneer curled his lip as it occurred to him that the mule skinner probably hadn't expected to see anyone either.

Murphy glanced over his shoulder at his victim. He knew he didn't need to worry about McCready interfering with his plans. He had gone to a great deal of trouble to get the emigrants this far and couldn't afford to let some nosy old mule skinner spook them just as he was preparing to spring his trap. With the old man out of the way, he didn't have to fret about the captain from Fort Laramie right away because the soldier was waiting for proof to back up McCready's suspicions before alerting his superiors.

Murphy caressed the talisman about his neck absent-mindedly. He had to locate that captain and silence him as he had the old skinner. Then, once he had his turn with that Rutheford girl, he intended to head back to Texas.

The pilot ripped the canvas coverings from two of the packages on the floor. He draped McCready over the mule's back, then threw the canvas over the corpse. He curled his meaty fingers around the mule's halter and gave it a sharp tug. The animal followed him outside. Man and animal trudged through the rain to the riverbank a little more than a hundred yards away.

At the river's edge Murphy uncovered McCready and hoisted him over his shoulder. He waded a couple of steps into the already swollen river before disposing of his burden in the swift current. Murphy watched the water carry the dead man into the main channel. Suddenly the body came to a halt, the churning, sand-filled water parting around it as though a rock had risen from the river-bed. Murphy swore, certain one of the sandbars in the shifting river bottom had snagged the old skinner. Well, he had no intention of slogging into the river and risking his life just to dislodge him. No one was likely to miss him for some time. And when they did, Murphy figured on being miles away.

# CHAPTER 4

"I'M grateful to you for seeing Jenny back to our wagon, Mr. Bailey," Carl Rutheford said, striking a match against the wagon box, then holding the flame to his pipe. He puffed deep and slow, until the blue-gray smoke rose above them, forming clouds among the bent hickory bows supporting the prairie schooner's canvas top. Rutheford shook out the match and tossed it outside through the opening at the rear of the wagon.

"It was my pleasure, sir," Cody assured him. "But I reckon I better get started back to the ranch."

"You have a ranch hereabouts?" Mrs. Rutheford asked.

"Well, no, ma'am. It's the Pony station—we just call it the ranch."

"Cody rides for the Pony Express, Mama," Jenny said, beaming at the young man.

"If you're from around these parts, then you know all about this talk of Indian trouble?"

Cody shook his head slowly. "Seems like there's always Sioux fightin' Pawnee. Pawnee fightin' Cheyenne. And once in a while one tribe or another fightin' the army. But there hasn't been a lot of that either. Biggest I ever heard of was the Harney Massacre back in 'fifty-five."

Rutheford took the pipe from between his teeth. "I recollect reading something about that. General Harney engaged a tribe of Sioux some miles west of here at a place called—"

"Ash Hollow."

"Yes, that's it. As I recall it was a barbaric attack. Women and children were killed right along with the Indian men."

27

"That made for hard feelin's, sure enough, but mostly between the Indians and the army. Not between Indians and emigrants."

Carl clamped his teeth on the stem of his pipe. "So this Indian scare is just a bunch of folks that have gotten the jitters?"

"I really don't know. All I can tell you is I haven't heard of one single attack from Fort Kearny to Fort Laramie. Now, to me, that sounds downright peaceful."

Carl Rutheford chuckled. "I must say I tend to agree with you, Mr. Bailey. A man in my situation, with a wife and a daughter to look after, likes things peaceful."

"Yes, sir, I reckon you would." Cody cleared his throat. "Well, I really got to get along."

"You're welcome to stay until the rain lets up," Mrs. Rutheford offered.

"Thanks, ma'am, but I do need to get back."

Actually Cody didn't like the idea of getting out in the storm, but he didn't want to offend the Rut#efords by telling them he felt cooped up in their wagon crammed full of boxes and trunks. He needed more room to breathe. He bade farewell to Mr. and Mrs. Rutheford, giving each of them a firm handshake. Finally the moment arrived when he had to tell Jenny good-bye. A heaviness filled his chest as he took her slender, delicate hand in his rough, calloused ones. He wanted to tell her how he wished they had met under different circumstances, but with her parents so close, he felt embarrassed even holding her hand.

"I'm glad I got to meet you," he said lamely.

She smiled, a sad, forlorn smile. "And I'm glad I got to meet you, Cody."

He held her hand for a moment longer, then clapped his hat on his head.

"Good luck to you all," he said, then hopped through the opening in the canvas. Mud sprayed from beneath his boots as he landed in the street. He pulled his hat down tight and made for Hanzel's Livery. He had an oilcloth poncho and an extra shirt in the bedroll on Champion's saddle. At least his top half would stay reasonably dry during the ride back to the Pony station.

When Cody reached the livery stable, Champion wasn't at the hitch rail where he had left him. He went into the barn, figuring the smith had taken Champ inside.

"Herman?" Cody hooted as he stepped through the doorway of the long stable.

"Dat you, Bailey?" Hanzel called as he emerged from one of the stalls that lined the east side of the barn.

"Yo! You got Champ in here?"

"Shore do. You gon ride out in dis storm?"

"Yeah. I want to get back before dark settles in."

"Ain' gon git much darker."

Cody walked into the stable.

"All the more reason to get goin' now. Isn't anything to keep me in town."

Despite the storm, Cody made no effort to hurry back to the Pony station. He couldn't help feeling a rare opportunity had eluded him. The foolish notion of something meaningful developing between him and that emigrant girl kept cropping up in his mind. The stormy darkness failed to blot out the vision of her honey-colored hair, or the warm glow of her blue eyes. He chided himself for behaving like a lovesick schoolboy, but made no attempt to block her from his thoughts. If anything, he tried to imagine every detail about her, etching her deeply into his memory. He didn't expect to encounter a young lady like her again.

Once in a while when Cody sat down with the stockmen to swap their exaggerated tales of adventure, the talk inevitably rolled around to women. The stock handlers, though not much older than himself, bragged of their escapades with many an erring lass, ribbing Cody at the same time for his lack of experience with the ladies. He took the good natured kidding without rancor. He never told them, or anyone, that his pa had raised him to believe the good Lord put one particular woman on earth for each man. And when a man dallied with women of ill fame he risked missing that special woman intended just for him. Cody didn't share his pa's teaching with his comrades because he figured they wouldn't understand. He wasn't sure he did.

The light from Silas's office appeared ahead through the sheets of rain. Cody rode into the ranch, heading for the stable, and dismounted at the entrance. Opening the door, he led Champion inside.

"Well, if it ain't the prodigal come home," Silas's head stockman John Butler called.

"Howdy, John."

"Boy, you ain't gonna get another saddle on old Champ if you're gonna ride him around in this kind of weather. He probably thought you's out huntin' the ark."

Cody led the mustang to his stall, then stripped off his saddle and blanket. He gave the horse a vigorous rubdown with the saddle blanket, then began combing him.

"Big doin's in town, I expect?" Butler asked, sauntering over to Champ's stall. He came to a halt, grasping the handle of his pitchfork like a staff.

Cody shrugged. "There was a crowd of folks, I reckon. Don't know as I've ever seen Wilkes's store so packed."

"That right? Everson doin' quite a business?"

"No more'n usual. Most folks was in for supplies, not liquor."

Butler laughed as he pushed his shoulder-length brown hair behind his right ear, then his left. He was a couple of years older than Cody, and laughing wasn't something that came easy to him. Most times he kept to himself, a silent and brooding figure. Cody had heard one of the other stockmen say that Butler had gotten into some kind of trouble back up the line, but Cody tried to shun gossip and had never asked Butler about it.

"Well, I guess I'll try and make up for that tomorrow when I go into the Junction."

"You're goin' in tomorrow?" Cody asked.

"Yep. Time for the supply run. Silas says it's my turn to go, but I swear I went last month."

"Want me to go with you?"

"Nah. Thanks anyway, but Everett said he'd go."

Everett Samuels had started working at the station a couple of weeks ago. He had come north after working for three years as a stock handler on the Butterfield line in Texas. Everett said little, keeping mostly to himself and the animals, but Butler considered him a first-rate stockman.

"I hope there's supplies left," Cody said, working the comb over Champion's flank.

"What d'ya mean?"

"Not only was there a passel of locals buyin' up ever'-thing with a price tag, there was a small train of emigrants in town, too."

Butler sat down on an empty nail keg and crossed his long legs. He scratched the end of his upturned nose as he leaned the pitchfork against the wall. "Emigrants, huh?"

Butler crossed his arms, his muscles bulging against the sleeves of his faded red cotton shirt. When he stood, he had five inches more height than Cody. He fixed his gaze on Bailey, a smile crinkling the corners of his deep-set brown eyes. "How small a train was it?"

"I don't recollect exactly. There may have been six or seven wagons. Why?"

"Some of them emigrants can have mighty pretty-lookin' ladies along. You know I've always had a real weakness for a pretty face."

Cody bristled. "They'll be pullin' out early. Probably be gone before you even get into town."

Butler knitted his brow. "Talk to 'em face to face, did ya?"

Cody cleared his throat nervously, averting his eyes from Butler's steady gaze.

"You keepin' somethin' from me, Cody? Your ol' pal?"

"I talked to one of them. She said—"

"She said? Whoa, boy, hold on a minute. You mean to tell me you got acquainted with one of them emigrant ladies?"

"We talked for a while."

Butler nodded his head slowly. "Talked, huh?" A mischievous light danced in his eyes.

"That's right!" Cody retorted. "We talked!"

Butler's eyes widened. "Settle down, Bailey. I ain't questionin' your purity. Lord knows, I've seen you preserve it enough. Is she the reason you're out ridin' in this storm?"

"I ain't interested in listenin' to your hazin', John."

"Hmm. I see she got to you. Are you in love?"

Blood rushed into Cody's face as he stepped from Champion's stall and stood in front of Butler. He liked John a lot. They had started working for Silas within a few days of each other. Being the two newest employees had created a special bond between them that had lasted ever since. At this moment, however, Cody was prepared to take his head off.

Right away Butler saw he had pushed Bailey far enough. He stood and reached for his pitchfork to feed Champion. "Didn't mean no harm. Ain't nothin' wrong with bein' in love."

"What would you know about it? Only women you ever been around sell their favors."

"Can't argue that," Butler said evenly. A smile parted his lips. "And that's the way I prefer it."

The humor returned to Cody's eyes. "I know that about you."

"Maybe you want to tell me about this girl?"

"Not right now," Cody replied, shaking his head. "I'm beat. I'm ready to hit the hay."

"Sure. Maybe we can talk tomorrow when I get back from town."

"Maybe."

Butler watched Cody amble from the barn; he had never seen him anger so quickly.

Cody trotted toward the sod bunkhouse, making no attempt to avoid splashing through the muddy pools that covered the yard. The rain still fell, but the severe storm had passed. Cody halted with his hand on the latch of the bunkhouse door. He glanced at the house and saw the lamplight behind the window of Silas's room. For a moment he considered going over there and talking to Silas about Jenny, but he rejected the notion. He had no idea how to convey what he felt to anyone. Anyone, that is, except Jenny. Maybe, he thought, she might feel the same way. But what did that matter now? Tomorrow she would be gone, and the day after that he had to ride.

Pushing the door open, Cody stepped over the threshold. Everett Samuels lay on the straw-filled tick of one of the rough-hewn bunks, reading a dime novel. In the bunk above him, another of Silas's stockmen, Orville Taylor, lay snoring with his face to the wall. Four other bunks lined the walls. One belonged to Cody and one to Butler. No one claimed the other two, although Silas insisted they would be filled as soon as he hired another rider and stock handler.

The bunkhouse had only one entrance and one window. Even on the sunniest day it remained dim and gloomy inside, as it had been built solely for the purpose of sleep. The single room contained the six bunks and one small round table with four chairs. A perpetual layer of dust covered everything, as unseen critters dislodged dirt while burrowing through the sod roof. The men preferred to spend most of their time outside, due as much to their disdain of the cramped, dreary quarters as to their like of the outdoors. Sometimes, however, the elements drove them to seek shelter in the cubbyhole.

"Evenin', Cody," the slim, blond Texan greeted.

"Howdy, Ev. Readin' a good one?"

Everett laid the book on his chest. "Fair. I see you got yer new guns."

Cody looked down at the Colts. He had almost forgotten about them. He had started to think the only reason he had gone to town today was to meet Jenny Rutheford.

He pulled the pistols from his sash. "Yeah, I got 'em all right."


Mary Rutheford made a pallet of quilts on the wagon floor as Carl squatted at the rear of the wagon, puffing on his pipe and peering out at the dwindling rain. Jenny had already curled up under a wool blanket near the front of the ten-foot wagon box and gone to sleep. Mary finished arranging the bedding, then sat on a crate near Carl.

"It will be so nice to have our own home again," Mary sighed as she folded her hands in her lap.

Carl nodded.

It had been hard for Mary to leave almost everything behind. They had wisely sold all of their furniture, rather than attempting to haul it across the wilderness. They had brought only those things necessary to sustain life on the trail and build a new home.

"Yes, it will," he agreed. He changed the subject. "I think young Mr. Bailey has a fair amount of knowledge about the savages in these parts."

"Then you think it's all right to keep going?"

"Yes, I do. We'll be fine. I purchased this wagon because I thought that false bottom could come in handy. If anything should happen we'll stick with our plan to hide Jenny there. But I don't think it will come to that."

Mary eyed him steadily.

"What is it, Mary?"

"Murphy."

He nodded slowly as he gazed into the growing darkness. "We don't have much longer before we reach Denver. It looks like we just have to put up with Mr. Murphy for a few more weeks."

"I don't understand," she said, shaking her head. "He seemed so capable. So, so—" She hesitated, searching for the right word. "Honorable?"

Carl smiled. "He took us all in, my dear. He seemed a most reliable man. And I'm sure he is. It's just that irascible disposition of his. No one saw it until we were well on the trail."

"I wish we could've found another pilot at the fort," Mary said.

Carl tapped his cold pipe against the tail of the wagon. "Well, there wasn't another to be had."

She didn't tell Carl she had noticed how Murphy gazed at Jenny whenever he got a chance. The sight of it filled her with disgust.

"Sometimes I think," she said, "we should be more concerned about Mr. Murphy than any savages."

"There, there now," Carl said.

"I suppose I should find some consolation in the fact that at least we outnumber the brute."

# CHAPTER 5

JOE Murphy had the emigrant train lumbering westward before sunup the next morning. He wanted as many miles between him and Parker's Junction as possible when they fished the mule skinner's body out of the river. Although he doubted anyone would connect him with the old man's murder, he had an important rendezvous to make and didn't want to get held up with a bunch of questions.

Once the sun had risen well above the horizon, Murphy informed the emigrants he was riding ahead to scout the trail. He ordered Jacob Carter, the driver of the lead wagon, to keep his oxen pointed due west. Then Murphy spurred his tall roan to a trot and headed west. As soon as the train dropped out of sight behind him, he turned his horse north to the river. Upon reaching the edge of the Platte he wheeled eastward, heading back toward Parker's Junction. He had ridden less than a mile when he approached a band of almost twenty riders. The point man halted the group when he spotted Murphy and broke away from the others to meet him.

"What's up, Joe?" Ike Pappas, a hard, rawboned Texan inquired as he reined his horse to a halt in front of Big Joe.

"We've run into some trouble."

"How's that?"

"The army's put some folks on our trail."

"The army?" Ike groaned. "We don't need this."

"Now, don't go yella on me, Ike. There's a mule skinner workin' with 'em, but I already took care o' him back there in Parker's Junction."

"If he's took care of, what's the trouble?"

"Well, maybe if ya let me finish I'll tell ya." Murphy growled, squinting his left eye at Pappas.

Ike squirmed in his saddle. He had ridden with Big Joe a long time and had learned to recognize the signs of his wrath. And when that eye squinted it meant tread easy.

"Sure, Joe. Go ahead."

"There was a greenhorn captain workin' with that skinner and I didn't have a chance to get him. He was a sandy-headed fella with a handlebar mustache. Not quite six feet tall and a little on the lean side. I want ya to send Chester and three or four others back to that town to find him. And if he ain't there, ya tell 'em to get on his trail, 'cause I want him dead."

Ike nodded emphatically. "I'll see to it. But maybe I oughta send somebody else instead of Chester."

"Why?"

"He's been kinda grumblin' about the boys not gettin' to ride into town and get likkered up."

Murphy stroked his beard. "You go ahead and send him. Maybe we'll get lucky and that soldier boy'll take care o' Chester for us."

Ike smiled. "I'll send him."

"You be sure and tell him that when the shootin's done, I don't want any bodies left behind. None o' our people or that captain. Understand?"

"I'll see to it, Joe."

"I gotta be gettin' back. I'll see ya after sundown and we'll go over the plans for tomorrow."

All that day the oxen plodded faithfully forward in the stifling heat. The sun bore down upon the small troop of demoralized emigrants. They had failed once again to rid themselves of Murphy and had finally accepted they had no recourse but to follow him. None of the pilgrims thought Murphy was anything more than an obnoxious bully, except, perhaps, Mary and Jenny Rutheford. And even they had no idea what Murphy really planned for them.

That evening, as the families started their cooking fires with the buffalo chips collected during the day, Murphy rode out of camp, as was his usual custom. Everyone had come to the conclusion he didn't care for any company but his own. This night, however, Murphy had an appointment to keep. He rode to the river, then turned east again. He had ridden to within a mile of the Pony Express station at Cold Springs before coming upon a camp along the riverbank.

"Hello, in the camp!" Murphy bellowed.

"Hey, Big Joe!" a voice called from the darkness.

"You the night guard, Dennison?" Murphy asked as he watched a gangly man cradling a shotgun approach.

"Yeah, that old gunrunner Pappas gave me the first watch."

"Is Pappas in camp?"

"Sure is."

Murphy spurred his horse past the sentry and rode into the camp. A blazing fire burned near the center of the camp and about fifteen men lay on blankets or sat against their saddles around the dancing light. Chester and his men hadn't returned. Several rose as Murphy entered the camp.

"We been waitin' for ya, Joe," Ike Pappas said as he stepped in front of the others. "We're all bankin' on a rich one."

Murphy swung down from the deep-chested roan, handing the reins to one of the men.

"Should be a good haul, Ike. There's a coupla farmers in the bunch, but mostly storekeepers lookin' to make a killin' sellin' goods in the Jefferson Territory. Reckon they'd need plenty of money to do that."

"Come on over and grab a cup of coffee," the lean-limbed Texan invited.

"Is it hot?"

"Hot and strong enough to float a wedge."

Murphy took a tin cup offered by one of the men and let Ike pour him a cup of the steaming coffee.

"Had any supper? Still some beans in the pot."

Murphy shook his head as he retreated from the heat of the fire. He squatted on his haunches and sipped his coffee. Ike knelt on one knee beside him.

"Have ya seen the money, Big Joe?"

Murphy's eyes peered over the lip of his cup, sweeping over the hungry faces gathered around him. "I seen enough to know it's there."

"Well, even if they ain't got no money, they're bound to have lotsa truck we could sell—"

"No!" Murphy interrupted as he stood and pitched his coffee into the fire. "That's what brought the law down on us back home. We don't take no wagons, we don't take no clothes. Nothin'! Nothin' but money and we burn what's left." He let his eyes rove over the men, studying each one. "And nobody walks away. I want no witnesses."

Ike stood slowly, shaking his head as though he couldn't comprehend what he had heard.

"Ever'body, Joe?"

"No witnesses. We already got some trouble and we don't need more."

"What trouble is that?" one of the men asked.

Murphy and Ike exchanged glances.

"The army. I ran into a nosy old skinner yesterday who was workin' for the army. He was on our trail."

The men began grumbling, exchanging uneasy glances.

Murphy's temper flared. "What'sa matter with y'all?" he demanded fiercely. "You needin' to hunt up somethin' for a backbone? I took care of him, but the job ain't finished.

There was an army captain with him and Ike sent Chester and a few others back to take care of him."

"What happens when they catch up with him?" a voice inquired from the fluttering shadows of the firelight.

"I gotta spell it out for ya?"

No one responded.

"Good. That's more like it. Now, the rest of you boys get on about yer business. I wanna talk to Ike. He'll fill ya in on what ya need to know in the mornin'."

The men drifted away from the campfire, breaking off into small pockets of two or three and speaking in hushed voices.

Murphy led Ike out of the camp. The two men walked in silence until they came to the riverbank. Murphy sat down, stretching his legs in front of him. Ike squatted next to him.

"Next time we do one of these jobs, I want you to be more careful. If any of them pilgrims had any savvy they'd a spotted ya a hunnerd times today."

"I was tryin' to be careful," Ike said.

"Figure we'll head back to Texas when this is done," Murphy said, ignoring Ike's remark. "I want ya to tell me which of these squareheads is worth takin' along."

"Sure. There's some good ones in this bunch."

"Well, I wanna be sure we take the Texas boys back home with us, but don't pick too many of the new ones. I wanna trim things back some."

"All right, Joe."

Somewhere on the other side of the river a coyote began its forlorn yipping. A cool breeze blew across the Platte, a soothing replacement for the humid afternoon.

Ike sat next to Murphy, studying his face, waiting for Murphy to speak.

"Tomorrow," Murphy said, "when you boys hit the train I want ya to save a package for me."

"Package?"

"Yep." He reached inside his shirt and withdrew the golden medallion. He gazed upon it, almost whispering the instructions he gave to Pappas. "There's a little yellow-haired girl, belongs to the tail wagon, and I want ya to see that no harm comes to her. I've had my eye on her quite some time."

Ike bobbed his head. "I'll see to it, Joe."

"Good. Now, ya better get back there and pump some nerve into these mama's boys. Them ignorant pilgrims'll be stranded not long after sunup and I want ya to be sure the boys understand I meant what I said about nobody bein' left alive when the deed's done tomorrow."

"They'll understand."

Murphy stood, stuffing the talisman back into his shirt, and started back to the fire, Pappas on his heels.

"They better . . ."


"Well, she's busted, Franklin," Murphy said as he crawled out from under Ted Franklin's wagon. "Ya lost a bolt and that axle come loose. I sure don't know where we're gonna find a tree out here to make ya a new one."

"I don't understand it," Franklin said, turning to Carl Rutheford. "I know I checked that axle just a few days ago. It looked fine then."

"Probably them buffalo runs we crossed yesterday afternoon," Murphy observed. "Man, when them runs are packed that hard they'd just about jar your teeth loose."

Carl Rutheford patted Ted's shoulder. "It's all right. We'll find something. Yours can't be the first broken axle out here."

"Well, I tell ya what," Murphy said. "Y'all get started unloadin' this wagon and I'll see if I can hunt somethin' up that'll at least get us to Julesburg."

"I'll get my axe and come with you," Carl offered.

"That ain't necessary. You stay and keep an eye on

things here. If I ain't found somethin' by noon, I'll be back and we'll have to cut this wagon in half."

"Oh, no," Luella Franklin sobbed.

Murphy shrugged. "I'm sorry, Miz Franklin," Murphy said with the most compassion any of them had ever heard from him. "We can't just stop here forever. It's a sad thing, but like Mr. Rutheford here said, ya ain't the first ones this ever happened to."

He sauntered to his horse and climbed into the saddle. "Y'all get started unloadin'," he said, then wheeled his horse and started away from the train.

Carl and Mary Rutheford stood together, watching him go as the others started emptying the Franklins' wagon.

"What do you make of that?" Mary asked.

"I'm not sure," Carl replied, shrugging. "It's like a different man took over Murphy's body."

Carl went to assist with the unloading, but Mary didn't move, her eyes fixed on the departing pilot.

"Is something the matter, Mary?" Luella Franklin asked as she came to stand beside her.

"Ever since we started this trip that man has grown increasingly cantankerous. So what has happened to change his disposition? I just don't understand."

"He's an odd one. That's for sure."

When Murphy had disappeared from the western horizon she turned her eyes on Carl. Sweat soaked his shirt as he lent Jacob Carter a hand carrying a long, heavy crate of farm tools.

"I guess we better get to helping these menfolks," Mary said.

Murphy had gradually led the pilgrims south since the train left Parker's Junction, until now the Platte Road lay nearly five miles north of their present position. He had wanted to get them away from the main road to avoid any chance meetings with army patrols or freighters or any other emigrants. He needed to have them isolated from any possible source of assistance.

The train had halted in a shallow basin on a wide plain, the wagons strung out in single file. They made an easy target. If any of them attempted an escape, the empty prairie offered few hiding places.

Murphy hadn't looked back until he was sure he had disappeared from the view of the train. Then he stopped and dismounted. He congratulated himself for laying a flawless trap as he loosened the cinch on the roan. He expected Ike and the rest of the boys to make short work of the pilgrims. He doubted any of the storekeepers or farmers had had much experience with firearms, outside of hunting. Without someone to coordinate their defense, their efforts would be in vain.

Murphy fished in one of his saddlebags for a chaw of jerked beef. He stretched out on the ground and bent his elbow so he could rest the back of his head on his forearm. He figured to lie here about an hour, then start for the rendezvous on the South Platte, just east of Freemont Springs. Then he aimed to head back home to Texas. At least three years had passed since he had plied this trade down there. He had plundered many a caravan since the early days of the California Gold Rush and murdered more people than he could count.

Sometimes he and his men had masqueraded as Indians to throw the authorities off their trail. They had used that ploy this time. Ike had sent several of the men riding over the surrounding countryside adorned in Indian garb to get folks stirred up. From what he had seen at Parker's Junction, the ruse had worked. Once the charred remains of the wagon train were discovered, everyone within a hundred miles would blame the Indians.

Only one loose end remained. The army captain. Murphy had lived long enough to know that even the best laid plans sometimes went awry. But if Chester and his men failed, Murphy fully intended to kill the captain himself. As long as the soldier lived, they all remained in danger.

Carl Rutheford mopped the sweat from his brow with the white cotton handkerchief he carried in his trouser pocket. It had taken half an hour of vigorous labor to empty the Franklins' wagon. He surveyed the possessions scattered around the prairie schooner. It would take a lot more time to reload it.

He took out his pipe and began filling the bowl with coarse tobacco. He sat down on one of Luella Franklin's oak ladderback chairs and proceeded to light his pipe. He had just started puffing when Jacob Carter stepped in front of him.

Carl looked up at him, but Jacob's eyes stared at something past Carl. Rutheford turned in his chair to see a cloud of dust ascending into the air. At the base of the cloud he saw a roiling mass of horses and riders.

"Get to your wagon, Jacob," he said as he stood. "All of you! Get to your wagons. You men get your guns ready, but don't shoot until we find out what they want."

Mary ran to her husband's side. Their eyes met. She threw her arms around his neck.

"I love you, Carl."

"I love you, too, Mary," he said, wrapping his arm around her waist and holding her tightly. He kissed her hard. "You better see to Jenny."

She nodded and fled to their wagon.

# CHAPTER 6

CHESTER Hailey had gotten his orders the previous day after Murphy intercepted the gang along the trail and parleyed with Ike Pappas. Ike picked five men to ride back to Parker's Junction with Chester, then gave them their instructions about what to do when they found the soldier.

"Big Joe says ya ain't to take no chances. Ya find this here yahoo and ya kill him. Understand?"

Chester Hailey shrugged. "What's not to understand. Reckon we can handle this, huh, boys?"

The others grunted their agreement. They had no reason to expect any trouble from a lone army captain.

"I don't think I need this many men, Ike. Reckon I could get the job done myself."

"Best just to do as yer told, Chester."

Chester shook his head in amazement. He had only ridden with Big Joe and Ike a few months, but already he had voiced his dissent several times regarding the way they managed things. He took every opportunity to badmouth Murphy and Pappas to the others when they weren't around. He had proclaimed himself a superior leader on numerous occasions, but he had yet to make a move to prove his assertions.

The outlaws rode into Parker's Junction early that evening. Chester swung his lanky frame out of the saddle at the hitch rail in front of Everson's saloon. His yellow lizard eyes studied the layout of the town. He removed his slouch hat, combing his oily black hair with his fingers as he let his gaze rove up and down the main street.

"Ed and Mac, check out that general store up the street

45

there," he said, waving with his hat towards Wilkes's.
"Woody, you and Matt head across the street to that saloon
and me and Frank will have a look in here," he said as he
hitched his thumb at Everson's.

"Let me do the talkin'," he said to Frank as the pair
stepped through the saloon's doorway.

"Evenin', gentlemen. What'll it be?" Bob Everson asked.

"Beer cold?" Chester inquired.

Everson shrugged.

"Nope. Sorry. But the whiskey'll sure stand you up."

Chester smiled. "Better have us a bottle then."

Turning his back to the bar, Chester rested his palms on
its edge as he surveyed the saloon's interior. Few customers
sat at the rough-hewn tables in the saloon, and he saw no
one that matched the description Ike had given them.

"Can I get you anything else?" the barkeep asked as he
served the whiskey.

"I was wonderin'," Chester said, facing Everson. "Have
you seen a slim, sandy-headed fella around here? He
sports himself a fine lookin' handlebar mustache."

It didn't take Everson long to think about it. He had
rented a bed to a man fitting that description for the past
three days. The man had left around noon that day.

"As a matter of fact, a man who looked just like that
checked out this mornin'. Folks was kinda wonderin' if he
had anything to do with the old skinner hauled outa the
river today. Is he a friend of yours?"

Chester shot a smile at Frank. "Yeah. You could say that.
Do ya know which way he's headin'?"

Everson shook his head. "West, I think, but I didn't
really see him leave."

"What's that about findin' an old skinner?" Frank asked.

"Darnedest thing," Everson said, shaking his head.
"Couple gents fished him out of the Platte this afternoon.
He'd been beat somethin' awful."

"Can be a hard country sometimes," Chester observed.

"That's a fact," Everson said. "Well, you boys gonna be spendin' the night? I got some real comfortable beds for rent upstairs."

"No, thanks, mister. We need to get on the trail. Appreciate it if you'd bring us another bottle to keep us company."

"Comin' right up."

Chester and Frank sauntered outside to the horses. Woody and Matt waited, each of them nursing a bottle of whiskey they had procured at the saloon across the street.

"Well, looks like this trip was worthwhile after all," Chester said with a chuckle as he displayed his own bottle. "If nothin' else we got to burn off some trail dust."

He tipped the bottle to his lips, taking several long gulps.

"Did you boys find out anything?" he asked as he wiped his mouth with the back of his hairy hand.

"Coupla folks seen him around," Woody said. "But that was 'bout it. . . . Here comes Ed and Mac."

"What's goin' on here?" Ed demanded as he moseyed up. "I hope ya got one of them bottles for me and Mac, seein' as how we had to walk the furthest."

"Tell us what ya found out, then you can go buy one for yourselves," Chester growled.

"The fellar bought some grub at that store this afternoon, then headed west. Didn't say where he was goin', but he was ridin' a dun with three black stockin's."

Chester nodded and smiled.

"Good work, Ed. Get your likker, then we'll get on this soldier boy's trail. I think it's a safe bet he's headin' for the army post. If we get movin' maybe we can get this business over with and join up with the others before they hit that train tomorrow."

They rode until sundown without encountering Captain Phillip Conway. A loathsome humor descended on Chester as the shadows lengthened across the desert.

"I sure didn't think it would take this long to find that

blue skunk," Chester growled irritably, feeling the effects of the liquor he had drunk and the long day spent in the saddle.

As the sun settled on the horizon he dispatched Ed and Mac to scout the surrounding country for signs of the trooper's encampment. The two had launched into a protest, but the venomous stare from Chester's yellow eyes had quickly quieted them. They had ridden out of camp, grumbling under their breath.

Frank and Woody scoured the prairie, searching for buffalo chips to fuel the campfire while Matt prepared a pot of coffee.

"I figger he's on this side the river," Ed said as they rode along the bank.

"Reckon that makes sense."

"We'll just ride along nice 'n' easy then. He ain't got no reason for thinkin' anybody's follerin' him, so he's likely to have him a nice fire."

"He oughta be pretty easy to spot," Mac said as he grinned.

Less than two hours had passed when Ed spotted the glow of a campfire. "I'd say that's where we want to go."

"Why don't we just sashay in there and be done with it?" Mac asked as he patted the revolver in his cross-draw holster.

Ed squinted at the fire in the distance, scratching his stubbly jaw. "That thought crossed my mind. That trooper oughta be easy pickin's if we ride in there real quiet like and catch him off guard. Then we can get back to Chester and try and catch up with Ike. . . . Yeah, all right, Mac, I'll go along with ya. But I'll make the first move. Agreed?"

Mac nodded. "Won't hear no argument from me."

Captain Phillip Conway had just settled against his saddle when he heard the unhurried plodding of Ed's and Mac's horses. He reached underneath his saddle, drawing out his Army Colt, then stood. He thrust the pistol into the waistband of his fringeless buckskin pants before squatting by the fire. He filled his battered tin cup with coffee from the pot nestled against the coals, then rose again.

"Hello, in the camp!" Ed hollered. "Room for a coupla fellow travelers?"

"Come on in," came the reply.

The two bandits dismounted and led their animals into the light of the campfire.

Conway ran his eyes over the men and their outfits and he saw right away they carried no packs or saddlebags. He nonchalantly inspected their soiled clothes and dust-covered boots. The condition of their garb indicated they had spent a great deal of time in the saddle over the last few days.

"You boys look like you've traveled a piece. Got ya a camp hereabouts?"

"Naw, we's ridin', lookin' for a spot when we seen yer fire," Ed replied.

"Coffee's hot," the captain said, extending the cup in his right hand toward the pot. "Help yourselves."

"Why that's right kind of ya," Mac said, starting for the fire. "How 'bout it, Ed? Gonna have a cup?"

The captain wrapped his hands around his cup as he lifted it to his lips. Gazing over the fire at the interlopers, he took a small sip, then lowered the cup. However, he now grasped it in his left hand rather than his right.

"You'll have to get your own cups. I've just got the one here."

Mac and Ed exchanged an anxious glance.

Conway's eyes narrowed as he watched them.

For a long moment no one moved and the only sound was of the crickets out in the darkness.

Suddenly the revolver materialized out of nowhere into the palm of Ed's hand. In motions excruciatingly slow,

Conway grabbed for the gun in his waistband as he lunged to his right. The pistol bucked in Ed's hand and flame leapt from its muzzle.

As the bullet slammed into the soldier's shoulder, twisting him away from the fire, he clutched the Colt in his fist and squeezed the trigger. He had targeted Ed, rightly viewing him as the immediate threat, but the impact of the slug skewed his aim so that his shot ripped a hole through Mac's windpipe.

The outlaw's eyes bulged in their sockets as his hands seized his throat. Mac sagged to his knees as blood seeped through his fingers and a low gurgling emanated from beneath his hands. He pitched forward into the dust as Ed's pistol roared again. He had taken more careful aim this time and the hot lead smashed into the trooper's left breast.

A sharp gasp escaped Conway's mouth as the second slug flattened him on the ground. The soldier gazed through the flickering campfire to see the outlaw's silhouette among the flames like a demon ascending from the depths of the abyss. He raised his head, lifted the Colt and fired twice.

Ed's face contorted in pain and surprise when the first bullet splintered his breastbone. He had been sure he'd killed the captain. The second ball penetrated his belly just below his ribs. The gun tumbled from his fingers as he doubled over and pitched face forward into the fire.

Conway laid on his back, breathing heavily, the stench of Ed's burning hair and flesh filling his nostrils until he nearly retched. Blood drenched the left side of his shirt and he fought to keep from losing consciousness. He had no way of knowing whether or not these men had come alone or if there were others waiting for him in the darkness. But the seriousness of the captain's wounds demanded that he seek some kind of help. He had passed the Cold Springs Pony Express station a few days before on his way to meet Pop McCready in Parker's Junction. It lay only a few miles further along the trail and was the nearest place where he could expect to find assistance.

He untied the gold sash around his waist, then stuffed it over the wounds inside his shirt. After rolling onto his stomach he lay still in an effort to catch his breath. Struggling onto all fours he crawled to his saddle. With barely enough energy to stagger to his feet, Conway dispensed with saddling his horse. He retrieved his war bag, which contained shot, powder flask, and caps, from beneath the saddle, then headed for his horse. The captain leaned against the animal a few moments in an effort to catch his wind. Finally, he managed to haul himself onto the steed and turn him west toward the Pony station.

"They've been gone nearly four hours, Chester. Maybe they run into trouble," said Woody.

Chester scowled. He had settled down for the evening to finish off the bottle of whiskey he had purchased earlier. "Ed and Mac are growed men, Woody. I got no inclination to saddle up again tonight and go huntin' for 'em. They probably just decided to hole up somewhere till mornin'. Anyway, if they run into that trooper I'm sure they can handle him with no help from us. Ain't no reason to get everybody all stirred up 'cause they ain't here."

Woody shrugged as he kicked at the dirt with the toe of his scuffed boot.

"Well, maybe it's 'cause they didn't take none of their outfit with them. I mean, they can't even make a cup of coffee."

Chester grimaced as he eyed Frank and Matt.

"Well, if y'all want to go on some bootless errand, huntin' men who don't need huntin', go right ahead. As for me, I'm stayin' right here by the fire with this bottle."

"I'll take Frank along with me, then."

Chester tipped the bottle to his lips as he gave Woody a wave of dismissal.

It didn't take Woody and Frank long to find their slain comrades. The foul odor of burnt flesh reached them long before they saw the flickering campfire. They had approached the camp cautiously, guns drawn, uncertain about what awaited them in the light ahead.

Frank spotted the two bodies lying near the fire and saw that one of them had fallen into the flames. He spotted Ed's Mexican spurs.

"Oh, lordy," Frank breathed.

"What is it?"

"Ol' Ed's face is burned pert near clean off."

The two men inspected the camp, revolvers at the ready. They found Conway's saddle and other belongings on the opposite side of the fire from the bodies of their confederates. They couldn't help noticing·the dried blood smeared on the saddle or the droplets of dried blood that they followed to the spot where Conway had picketed his horse.

Woody knelt on one knee, studying the tracks leading into the desert. He suddenly sprang to his feet.

"What? What is it?" Frank demanded.

"I got a feelin' this was our man and he's headed west. Get back to Chester and tell him what we found here."

"Where're you goin'?"

"I'm goin' after him," Woody said, pointing at the hoofprints in the dust.

# CHAPTER 7

THE light of the distant dawn painted a sliver of brilliant gold along the horizon. Cody stood outside the station office, straining his ear for the sound of pounding hoofs that heralded the approaching Pony rider. He clutched the reins of Champion's bridle in his fist.

The mail from the east was already several hours late. Normally Cody made his ride during the night, but as of yet he had seen no sign of an incoming rider. Such a delay was highly irregular.

Suddenly Champion lifted his head and pricked his ears. Cody caught the movement. He closed his eyes tightly, turning his head to the prairie as if the action would improve his hearing. Within seconds he heard the thunder of hoofs on the flinty plain.

He spun on his heel to check the cinch one last time. He didn't use his own saddle, but a stripped-down, lighter model provided by the company. The incoming rider would dismount, jerk the mochila from his saddle, and toss it to Cody.

The mochila, a leather square not much larger than a saddle blanket, had two holes cut into its middle. The saddle horn fit through the smallest one and the other hole slipped over the cantle. When a Pony rider mounted, his legs and seat would hold the mochila firmly in place. In each corner of the leather blanket was a cantina, a rectangular pouch for the mail, one in front of each leg, and one behind each leg. Three of the pouches carried correspondence. The fourth contained a time card for recording arrivals and departures at various stations. A small brass padlock held the individual cantinas closed and every stationmaster had a key to the fourth cantina. However, the others could only be opened at the forts along the route and in St. Joe or Sacramento.

Cody spotted a dark figure racing toward the station. When the Pony Express was first started, the company had issued a small bugle to each rider, with instructions to blow it loud as they neared a station. It didn't take long before everyone realized the pounding of the horses' hooves provided sufficient alarm and the bugles disappeared.

John Butler came out of the bunkhouse, one suspender hitched over his left shoulder, the other dangling against his leg. He vigorously scratched the top of his head as he sauntered across the yard to Cody.

"Ready to ride?" Butler called to Cody.

"Yep. Looks like Billy Holden's finally comin' in."

Butler turned his gaze to the east as he came to a halt beside Cody. He looped the other suspender over his right shoulder, his eyes on the approaching rider.

"You got plenty of powder?"

"Enough to get the job done, I reckon." Cody looked at Butler. "You ain't turnin' into old Silas, worryin' about Indians, are you?"

"I don't know about Indians, but there sure was quite a commotion in town yesterday afternoon. You'd already turned in when me and Everett got back, so I didn't get a chance to tell you last night."

"Tell me what? Were there more people buyin' out Wilkes?"

"I ain't talkin' about people buyin' anything. Seems some old fella got his head stove in before he was pitched into the river. Somebody said they thought he was a mule skinner. Everson said he had seen you talkin' to him just the day before."

Cody's eyes widened. "Heavy fella? Not much taller than me?"

"Can't say. I never saw him. Only two things I know about him is he's a stranger and he's dead," John replied with a shrug, his eyes studying the incoming rider. "You're up, Cody."

Billy sped into the station as the words left Butler's mouth. He swung off his horse before his mount had come to a halt, seizing the mochila as he leapt from the saddle. He pitched it to Butler, who threw it onto Champion's back.

"Runnin' late, Billy. Have some trouble?" Butler asked as he fit the mochila onto the saddle.

"Naw. It's too quiet for an undertaker," Billy replied. "But Newt Morley's horse busted it's leg comin' outa Fort Kearny. Whole schedule's shot."

"We'll do our best to get it back on line," Cody said as he grasped the saddle horn and mounted.

Butler gave Champion a hard slap on the rump. The mustang knew the routine and bolted for the prairie. Usually Cody relished these rapid exits, but this morning that brief conversation with Butler had unsettled him. The dead man could only be Pop McCready. He wanted to turn Champion around and ride back to the Junction and find out what had happened, but he knew he couldn't. He had taken an oath to see to his duties. The mail had to go through. Any inquiry had to wait until he returned. He leaned low over the horn and with his quirt gave Champion two quick raps on his flanks. The gelding took the signal and stretched out, his legs churning.

Cody squinted against the wind as he stared between Champion's ears. He felt the warmth of the rising sun on his back as they charged across the plain. Cody would reach the next station in less than an hour and change mounts there, so he didn't hesitate to drive Champion hard. Besides, the lithe mustang loved running full out.

★ ★ ★

Captain Phillip Conway lay in the tall grass, his horse grazing nearby. He had halted after becoming lightheaded and nearly falling off his mount. Once his equilibrium returned, he began reloading his pistol. He rolled onto his side, then pushed himself to a sitting position. He saw the pale pink of the coming dawn on the distant horizon. He would die if he didn't get to a doctor soon. The wound in his shoulder was hardly more than a crease and had stopped bleeding, but the gunshot just below and to the left of his left nipple looked bad. The ball had penetrated his lung and, near as he could tell, hadn't exited.

He had just snapped the rammer into place when the dun lifted its head, pricking its ears. Conway lay on his stomach and listened closely to the prairie, but only heard his own rasping breath. The dun had definitely heard something, for the horse still stood motionless.

In spite of the cool morning, sweat glistened on Conway's forehead. He licked his lips, cursing himself for not thinking to bring his canteen. The captain wiped his forehead with his shirt sleeve.

Suddenly he heard the muffled hoof falls. And just as abruptly they were still. The gaze of his steed remained fixed on the horse that the tall grass obscured from Conway's sight. He listened intently as the sound of creaking saddle leather reached his ears. He couldn't see if anyone had dismounted. Again he looked to the dun for his answer and saw the animal had returned to its grazing.

Scouring the prairie for some sign of the captain, Woody had spotted the riderless dun. Woody had scouted ahead of the others and now stood in his stirrups to search the surrounding desert, a prudent maneuver when approaching the unexpected, and even more so in the wilderness. He saw nothing else as his eyes swept over the endless plains. The dun ignored him and returned to cropping the seemingly endless supply of grass.

Suddenly Conway heard the low rumble of advancing horses.

Woody heard them too. He removed his hat as he turned in his saddle.

"Over here!" Woody called as he waved.

In the dim gray morning Conway spied a hat waving above the tops of the grass. He slowly came to his knees and saw the man signaling to his compatriots, holding his hat aloft. The captain moved into a crouching position and began backing away from the stranger and toward the dun.

"Did ya find him?" The call sounded distant.

"Just his horse!"

"Murphy don't want the horse!"

The captain's eyes widened at the mention of Murphy's name. Conway had reached the dun, when suddenly his eyes met the scout's.

The outlaw flung his hat down, clutching frantically for his holstered pistol, but Conway already had him in his sights and pulled the Army Colt's trigger.

The bullet struck Woody beneath his collar bone and toppled him from his horse's back.

Gunfire erupted behind him as the captain swung onto the dun's back. He dug his heels into the animal's flanks, sending him galloping across the prairie.

Woody sat up, holding his hand against his wound. He stood unsteadily, then staggered to his horse, grabbing hold of the saddle horn. He had just managed to clamber up when Chester Hailey rode up with Matt and Frank.

"Did ya get him?" Chester demanded.

Woody shook his head. "Never got off a shot," he said panting.

"Can ya ride?"

"Sure I can ride."

"Well, let's get after him," Chester ordered. "We're close now. And I don't want to lose him again."

He dug his spurs into his horse. The animal reared, neighing in protest, then shot across the level in pursuit of the dun. The others rode into his dust.

Bob Lassiter plopped down on the empty nail keg that served as his chair and scooted it up to the table made of planks laid over two upended crates. Across the table Rafe Johnson and Tommy Graves had already started to work on their flapjacks and bacon. Jeb Larson, the stationmaster of the Cold Springs Pony Express station dropped a plate of the same in front of Bob.

"You get that hoss ready for Cody?" Jeb asked as he returned to the stove to fill his own plate.

Bob leaned over his breakfast and took in a deep breath, inhaling the mouthwatering aroma of fresh bacon and hot cakes. He grasped his knife and fork and dug in.

"Yup," Bob said around a mouthful of bacon. "I saddled that chestnut with the star on his forehead. Next to Champion, that's Cody's favorite horse."

Jeb chuckled as he poured himself a cup of coffee.

"Sometimes I wonder if Bailey thinks there is any other hoss 'cept that pinto of his."

The stationmaster had just set his cup and plate on the table when they heard the distant gunfire.

"Grab yer guns, boys!" Jeb ordered as he grabbed his double-barreled shotgun from the corner nearest the table.

The four men ran into the station yard, stopping near the stable, their eyes sweeping the horizon. More shots cracked through the air.

"They're comin' from the east," Tommy said.

Bob turned to Jeb.

"Could be Cody in trouble. Maybe I better ride out—"

"Nope. Them shots are comin' closer. If it's Cody he's still ridin'. We'll just hold our ground and be ready to back him up if need be."

"There!" Tommy yelled.

They followed his pointing finger and saw a rider rapidly approaching. Four other horsemen followed him.

"What do you make of it, Jeb?" Bob asked.

"Don't know. Reckon we'll find out pretty quick."

Captain Conway's dun galloped into the station yard and the captain leapt from its back, oblivious to the guns trained on him, and tumbled into the dust.

"Hold yer fire, boys!" Jeb commanded. "This fellar's all shot up."

The stationmaster knelt beside the wounded man.

"I'm Captain Phillip Conway, Fort Laramie," he gasped. "Outlaws after me." His eyes rolled back in his head.

"Is he dead?" Rafe asked.

"He oughta be," Jeb replied, shaking his head.

Suddenly a torrent of lead descended upon the station. Rafe Johnson crumpled to the ground, blood streaming from a wound in the center of his forehead.

"Get to the stable!" Jeb shouted as he drew his revolver and began returning the mounted outlaws' fire. "And grab the trooper!"

"Rafe!" Tommy hollered.

"Too late for him!" Bob yelled over the din of gunfire. He grabbed Tommy's sleeve. "Help me get the captain!"

Chester saw the three men break for the stable, dragging Conway with them. He had to get to them before they barricaded themselves inside. He didn't have time for a siege. He had to finish it now.

"C'mon, let's get in there!"

The four outlaws charged into the station yard, unleashing a hailstorm of bullets on the retreating station men.

Jeb reached the door to the sod stable first and leaned his shotgun against its facade. His hand closed on the handle as a bullet slammed into his back between his shoulder blades. The impact threw him against the door. He pushed himself back from the building, still clutching the handle, and flung the door open, then turned to cover Bob's and Tommy's retreat. He took two more bullets in his chest and another in his belly. The stationmaster gave as good as he got, knocking Woody from his saddle with a bullet through his eye and putting two slugs into Chester.

Crouching low, Tommy and Bob lugged the wounded soldier to the stable and made no attempt to return the outlaws' shots as they scrambled across the yard, covered by Jeb's fire. Then a bullet pierced Tommy's skull, hurling him to the ground, his arms flailing the air like a broken whirligig. Still clutching the captain's sleeve in his left hand, Bob turned the pistol he gripped in his other hand on the gunman and fired. The ball hit the outlaw's horse in the neck, causing it to rear with a crazed shriek.

Matt plunged to the dirt, landing on his left arm. He yipped like a wounded coyote as his arm snapped just below the elbow. He staggered to his feet, his arm dangling awkwardly at his side, but his gun still in his good hand. He leveled the pistol at Bob Lassiter and started shooting.

A slug ripped into Bob's back just as he reached the doorway and Jeb. The stationmaster grabbed hold of Conway's collar as the stockman's knees buckled, driving him to the sandy soil. Bob whirled around, taking another slug in his side as his own pistol blasted lead into Matt's shoulder.

Jeb dropped the unconscious officer onto the stable floor, then scurried outside to retrieve the shotgun, which he turned on Frank, the only outlaw unscathed in the fracas and who now brought his gun to bear on the stationmaster. Jeb let him have it with both barrels, blowing Frank out of his saddle.

"C'mon, Bob!" Jeb called out as he snagged the stockman's sleeve.

The two men managed to scramble into the stable, collapsing on the hard, cold earthen floor, gasping for air.

"Are you hit bad, Bob?"

"Purt near blown to pieces, Jeb. How 'bout you?"

"Same, I reckon. Think you can get to Bonner's? Bring back some help?"

Bob managed to pull himself up. He studied Jeb's blood-soaked shirt.

"You oughta think 'bout goin' with me."

"Naw. Somebody's gotta keep the captain here company. Wouldn't be proper to run off on a guest."

Bob looked at Conway, shaking his head.

"Jeb, this soldier boy's gotta be dead."

Jeb Larson shook his head.

"You look close you'll see he's still breathin'. And I ain't about to let them varmints get to him. 'Specially since they killed Rafe and Tommy. You gotta go, Bob. You gotta try and head off Cody."

Though hurting and bleeding profusely, Bob picked himself up from the floor and lumbered to the side door of the stable, which led into the corral. He cracked the door open and peered out. The chestnut he had saddled for Cody stood tied outside the rails where he had left it hardly twenty minutes earlier. Bob stepped into the pen and slid along the side of the soddy until he came to its front corner. He peeked around the edge of the building and saw the stunned and bloodied outlaws in the yard. None of them looked in his direction.

The stockman slipped between the corral bars and untied the pony. He turned the animal's off side to the yard, then boosted himself into the saddle. He slapped the horse with the bridle reins, hollering as loud as he could.

In the station yard only Chester remained on his horse, and he was hurt bad, hit by two bullets in his left breast. Woody lay dead, sprawled on his back, one eye shot out, the other staring blankly at the sky. Frank sat wounded in the dirt, arms folded over his belly and his chin resting on his chest. Matt stood a few short steps from the stable, weaving drunkenly. He had dropped his six-shooter and labored at stuffing his bandanna into his shirt in a vain attempt to stem the flow of blood from the hole in his shoulder.

"Can you boys get mounted?" Chester asked, his voice tight with pain.

"Mine's gone, Chester," Matt croaked.

"I'll need help to get mounted," Frank said without lifting his head.

"If I get down off this horse I ain't sure I could get back on him," Chester said, gazing at his wounded comrades.

Suddenly Chester heard Bob Lassiter's whoop.

"Dang, Chester! Shoot 'im!" Matt yelled.

Chester raised his pistol and pulled the trigger. The hammer clicked on an empty chamber. For a moment he stared helplessly after the rider.

"If he reaches help, we're gonna be in real trouble," Matt panted. "He'll bring a posse down on us for sure."

"Reckon you're right about that. We've got to get away as fast as we can. Help me get Frank on his horse. You push him from below, I'll pull from up here."

After a great deal of puffing and wheezing the two outlaws succeeded in getting Frank in his saddle.

"Before ya get mounted," Chester told Matt, "go open up that corral. We'll chase them horses off before we go."

The outlaws rode west from the Cold Springs station, headed toward the rendezvous with Murphy and the rest of the gang along the South Platte.

# CHAPTER 8

THE ten miles to Cold Springs station passed quickly. Cody rose in his saddle as the station came in sight and knew immediately that something was wrong. He pulled on Champion's reins as he closed into within a couple hundred yards of the station. The pony shook his head, unaccustomed to slowing this far from their destination. From this distance Cody had a clear view of the station yard, where one of the stockmen usually stood by the corral with his next mount, but this morning he saw three dark figures lying on the dusty ground.

Cody's fingers closed on the cool walnut handle of one of the Colts in his sash and he drew the weapon, holding it behind the saddle horn. Everything looked peaceful as his blue eyes searched the terrain around him, but he had learned long ago not to depend on just what his eyes could see. He listened to the land, hearing only silence, and sniffed like a wary hound. Whatever had happened here hadn't ended very long ago, for the sulfurous odor of spent gunpowder lingered in the still morning air.

He reined the mustang to a halt near the empty corral.

He knew the Indians in these parts admired the fine horseflesh Russell, Majors & Waddell had purchased for the Pony and weren't bashful about stealing them when the opportunity presented itself. The farther west a Pony station was located, the more it became a prime target for such raids. The planners of the express line had set up nearly one hundred and ninety stations, ten miles apart, and riders changed horses at each one. They also established home stations at intervals of approximately eighty miles for the changing of riders, as well as mounts. The distances between these outposts, and their generally isolated locations, increased their vulnerability to Indian and outlaw attacks.

Cody dismounted, firmly gripping the Colt in his right hand and Champion's reins in the other. He recognized the body closest to him as that of stockman Tommy Graves, his head laying in a wide pool of blood and flies buzzing all around him. Cody cocked his pistol as he warily approached the corpse of a man sprawled on his back. He had never seen this man before and it caused him to reconsider his first assumption that Indians had attacked the station. Outlaws were as much of a scourge, if not more, to the Express than the Indians.

Finally Cody reached the last dead man, stretched out facedown just outside the station headquarters. He turned the corpse over with the toe of his boot. Rafe Johnson, another of Jeb Larson's stockmen, had a gaping bullet hole in his forehead.

The Pony rider's eyes swept over the rolling prairie again as he secured his horse at the hitch rail that stood a few short steps from the entrance to the Cold Springs headquarters, a low soddy not much larger than the bunkhouse at Silas's. His gaze took in the empty corral and the three lifeless men, baking in the rising sun, then he turned and headed for the open doorway of the station house.

Built almost thirty feet square, the soddy consisted of one open room. Four unmade bunks filled the room to the right of the entrance. A cookstove nestled in the far corner to the left and next to it stood a crude table made of weatherbeaten planks laid across upended crates. Three smaller boxes and a short keg served as chairs. The dishes from breakfast sat on the table, still laden with food.

After completing his inspection of the room, Cody stood by the stove, tucking the Colt into his sash. He saw no sign of stationmaster Jeb Larson or stockman Bob Lassiter.

The situation puzzled him, but he knew he would have to leave further investigation to others. He had to deliver the mail. He would report this mystery to the company officials at Freemont Springs.

He heard Champion nicker outside and sidled up to the doorway. He spied a sandy-headed man hunched over by the hitching rail, fiddling with the mustang's reins.

Cody pulled a revolver and thumbed back the hammer. "Hold it, mister!"

The stranger's hands dropped to his side. "Don't shoot. I'm unarmed."

Cody stepped into the sunshine, noticing for the first time that the man's back was soaked with blood.

"Just step away from the pony, fella. And move real slow."

He edged back from the horse, then, holding his hands away from his body, turned to face Cody.

"Lord, mister, you're shot up bad."

"I'm Captain Phillip Conway of the United States Army out of Fort Laramie."

Cody studied the pale face with its sharp, angular features and sandy handlebar mustache. He released the hammer on his pistol. Whether the stranger told the truth or not, Cody knew he had nothing to fear. Death was on this man's trail.

"You better sit down here next to the house," Cody said as he shoved his gun into the band around his waist. He strode to the wounded man's side and took him by the arm, then helped him sit down against the wall.

"I've got to use your horse," he said, his breath coming raggedly.

"What happened here?"

"I'm Captain Phillip Conway and I've got to get to Fort Laramie. I need your horse."

Cody swept his hat off and squatted in front of the

dying man. Blood soaked the front of the captain's shirt and still oozed from several wounds in his chest and belly.

"Fella, you know you ain't goin' anywhere, don't you?"

Conway dropped his chin onto his chest and gazed at his bloodied shirt.

"Reckon I'm done for, all right," he said without lifting his head.

Cody glanced over his shoulder at Champion. He figured he had lost about thirty minutes' riding time poking around here. The mail was extremely late already and he needed to get on the trail. However, Bailey was reluctant to leave the dying captain, even though he knew he could do nothing for him.

A coughing spasm racked the soldier's body. Once it passed, he laid the back of his head against the wall, panting heavily.

"You're with the Pony Express?" he asked, gasping for air.

"That's right. I was supposed to change mounts here, but it looks like maybe Indians, or outlaws, done made off with all of the stock."

The captain's head swayed from side to side.

"Not Indians," he whispered. "Outlaws. Thieves, murderers. Came up from Texas. They're white men. Pop warned me. I wouldn't listen." Another fit of coughing erupted and Conway began spitting blood. He started to slide into the dust, but Cody caught him.

"Pop warned you? Pop McCready?" Cody asked, shocked.

The captain's eyes fluttered open. They darted back and forth, as if searching for something.

"Yes, McCready. You know him?"

Cody clapped his hat on his head. He knew Pop all right. He knew Pop was dead.

"Tell me what happened here."

"Attacked . . . sent a man for help."

"Anybody else around?"

"Dead. There's another man in the stable, dead."

"Who did you send for help?" Bailey knew the captain wouldn't last much longer.

"You've got to find Pop for me. Tell him he was right. . . . Murphy's our man. He's got to get word to Major Flynn."

Cody gasped. Murphy! He stared at the ground, shaking his head in disbelief. Pop had tried to tell him about the pilot, but what could he have done? Suddenly a deep despair overwhelmed him as he realized his answer to that question. He could have warned the Ruthefords. Cody felt sick to his stomach.

"I guess we both should have listened to Pop," Cody said as he raised his eyes, but he knew Conway didn't hear him.

Cody pulled the captain away from the side of the house. He dragged the dead man into the soddy and laid him on the floor. He did the same with Rafe Johnson's body, then crossed the yard to the stable, where he found Jeb Larson.

He laid out Tommy Graves and the stranger in the stable with Jeb. Someone would come back from the Freemont Springs station to bury them. Cody left the dead men inside.

He crossed the yard, halting just outside the doorway. He leaned against the house, gazing at the mochila on Champion's back. He had sworn an oath to see the mail went through, regardless of weather, Indians, or outlaws. For more than a year he had stuck by that oath, never once faltering in his job. It had nearly cost him his life once, when a blizzard had howled across the prairie, burying everything in its path, but he had gotten the mail through.

The sun climbed high in the clear sky, and Cody heard a hawk screeching overhead. He knew they would be expecting him in Freemont Springs pretty soon, but he kept thinking about Jenny and the look on her face that afternoon when Murphy had leered at her through the glass at Wilkes's store. He looked away from the mochila, scanning the plains to the south. She was out there somewhere and in danger. And who else knew? Not the army. Their man died before he could tell anyone else except Cody.

A light breeze stirred up a dust devil in the yard of the Cold Springs station. Cody had gained a deep appreciation for the quiet solitude of the endless desert. He loved this place. Out here in the wilderness things had changed little since men had first begun to explore its wonders. He had seen mighty forces at work here and had learned that ignorance in this land could be fatal without someone to guide you. And if that someone had it in mind to take advantage of you there was little to be done.

Finally Cody made up his mind. He would make sure the mail got to Freemont Springs, but someone else had to take it from there. He had to find the Rutheford train.

He strode to the hitch rail, untied Champion, and swung into the saddle, straddling the mochila. He spurred the mustang as he let out a whoop. The pony lunged into a gallop. Within moments both horse and rider had disappeared like a phantom of the desert.

# CHAPTER 9

JOHN Butler's head shot up as soon as he heard the advancing hoofbeats. He saw the rider coming in from the west and recognized right away that it wasn't Cody. As the horseman neared, John saw that he had difficulty staying in the saddle. As he stood, he dropped the bridle he had been repairing.

"Yo, Silas! Everett!" John hollered. "Rider's comin' in!"

Everett came around the side of the barn, followed by Orville Taylor, as Silas stepped through the door of his office.

"Can you see who it is?" Silas asked, coming up to Butler.

"I'm not sure, but it looks like Bob Lassiter."

"Lassiter? From Cold Springs?" Silas shook his head. "I don't like this. Looks like he's in trouble."

John nodded.

"He is, but he's gonna make it this far."

"Is it Cody?" Everett inquired as he and Orville reached the other two men.

"Nope," Silas responded. "Bob Lassiter from over at Cold Springs. Go into the house and get my bandage kit in the pantry. I got a feelin' that boy's gonna need some doctorin'. Orville, go with him and get some water boilin'."

The two men raced for the house as Lassiter's horse entered the yard. Both John and Silas reached the animal as Bob slipped from the saddle. They caught him and laid him on the ground.

"Oh, man!" John exclaimed.

"He's shot up pretty bad," Silas agreed. "It's a wonder he stayed in the saddle this far.

"Hurry up with that kit, Everett!" he called over his shoulder.

"Bob, can you hear me?" John asked, cradling Lassiter's head in his lap.

"Johnny?"

"Yeah, it's me. Silas is here too. Can you tell us what happened?"

Lassiter licked his lips as he nodded his head. Silas had already started to work, tearing away his bloodied shirt, when Everett returned with a scuffed and worn satchel.

"We was just sittin' down to breakfast when we heard a ruckus outside. Thought it was Injuns after Cody at first. We got out o' the soddy and this fella comes ridin' in, burnin' the breeze. He's all bloody and fell off his horse 'fore it even come to a stop. Said he's an army captain from Fort Laramie and outlaws was on his trail, then he passed out. I think he's dead."

Silas continued his futile efforts to stem the flow of blood from Lassiter's bullet-riddled body. He looked at John and shook his head, then turned to Everett.

"Better bring Bob some water."

"He'd hardly told us who he was 'fore it started rainin' lead," Bob continued. "They cut down Rafe in the first round. Jeb and Tommy and me broke for the stable, but Tommy never made it. Jeb told me to go for help, so I took the horse I'd saddled for Cody and hightailed it here. Don't reckon Jeb coulda held out very long. I wanted him to come with me."

"Did you see Cody?" John asked.

Lassiter's eyes rolled back before he could answer.

Everett came up with a dipper of water, but Silas shook his head.

"He won't be needin' it now."

John laid Bob's head on the ground, then raised his eyes to meet Silas's.

"I gotta find out what happened to Cody."

"That'll leave me short-handed, John."

"Everett and Orville can take care of things. And Billy Holden can help out when he gets back from town. Besides, the eastbound rider isn't due in for a couple days."

"If you're goin', I'm goin' with you," Everett said.

"Ain't nobody goin' anywhere right this minute," Silas growled. "You boys need to get a grave dug for Bob. When that's done we'll talk 'bout who's goin' after Cody."

"Cody could be in trouble right now," John protested.

"If he is, you're already too late to help him."

"No, I ain't. If he's lyin' out there on the trail with a few slugs in him, the sooner I get to him the better his chances'll be."

Silas cocked one bushy white eyebrow at Butler. "Well, I reckon somebody's got to go. After all there's the mail to think about. All right, Butler, you and Everett get mounted up. Me and Orville will see to Bob here."

John hopped to his feet.

"I'll cut out a coupla horses, Ev. Grab our gear," John called, already sprinting to the corral.

Everett headed for the barn.

"Be sure to load up with plenty o' powder and shot!" Silas called after Everett. He stood as he gazed at Bob's bloodied corpse. "I'd say it looks like yer gonna need it."

Within fifteen minutes John had cut out two horses from the corral and he and Everett had thrown their saddles on them. Orville brought each of them a sack of hardtack and jerked beef, then filled their canteens from the well.

"Wish I was goin' with you, boys," Orville groused, handing them the canteens.

"Yeah," John said as he swung aboard his golden-brown palomino. "But somebody's gotta stay here and help Silas look after things. Besides, if Cody comes back here before we find him, it falls to you to get the mail through."

Orville nodded.

"I reckon you'll find Cody all right," he said.

Everett mounted a tall black gelding and gathered the reins in his gloved hands. He looked at Orville.

"I hope so."

"Enough of this jawin'," John declared. "Let's ride."

He put the spurs to the palomino and the horse lunged from the station yard, with Everett on the black right behind him.

An hour later the two stockmen stood outside the soddy at Cold Springs. They had discovered the bodies of Jeb Larson and Tommy Graves in the stable, along with Woody's. In the station house they found Phillip Conway and Rafe Johnson.

"Huh! This is terrible," Everett said as he pulled off his hat and scratched his head. "I ain't never seen anything like this. What do you make of it?"

John shrugged his broad shoulders.

"I don't. We'll have to leave all of this till later. We gotta find out what happened to Cody."

"Head for Freemont Springs?"

John nodded.

"That's where he'd be ridin'."

Champion streaked over the plains, covering the prairie faster than wildfire. Cody hunched low in the saddle, his hat brim flapping against its crown. The road rose and fell beneath them as they dashed across the rolling landscape. Champion's hooves thundered on the hard road and his breath came in sharp gasps.

The Cold Springs station lay six miles behind them, and Cody expected to reach Freemont Springs in another twenty minutes. He had no doubts Champion could make the distance, and then some, but he intended to get another horse at the station. He had no idea how long he had to catch up to the Ruthefords and warn them, if indeed he wasn't too late already.

Suddenly he spied a towering column of black smoke, rising against the cloudless blue sky in the southwest. Without a second of doubt, or debate, he jerked the reins and turned Champion. They bounded into the shallow waters of the Platte and up the bank on the other side. With an explosive burst of speed, Champion surged across the level ground, aiming for the black pillar in the distance.

Fifteen minutes later Cody topped a rise and observed the desert pirates about their labor. Flames already engulfed four of the six wagons in the Rutheford's train. It sat in the basin of a wide plain less than a mile from Cody's position. He felt as if he were looking into a bottomless pit as he heard the screams of the victims and watched the mounted attackers riding to-and-fro like specters among the carnage they had created.

Cody's stomach churned as he fought down the vomit rising in the back of his throat. He spurred Champion down the low hill, knowing he had embarked on a fool's mission.

The outlaws had finished their business, setting fire to the final wagon, without even noticing the Pony rider's approach. As Cody closed in on the turbulent scene before him he saw the desperados commence their retreat. He didn't slow Champion, but headed for the last prairie schooner in the column, which he recognized as the Ruthefords'.

Flames had nearly consumed the canvas top and the bent hickory bows that had once held it aloft. The wagon box itself had just begun to burn. Cody reined Champion to an abrupt halt, nearly setting the horse on his rump. He leapt from the saddle, then froze, unable to believe the butchery in front of his eyes. Bodies lay strewn all around him. To his horror he saw that many had been scalped to give the appearance of an Indian attack. Clothing, tools, household goods, the contents of all of the wagons lay scattered over the plain. Cody bowed his head. He wanted to search among the bodies for Jenny, but he didn't dare, fearing what he might find. He had seen more death today than he had in all his life.

Cody spun on his heels and started for Champion. Once he delivered the mail to Freemont Springs and reported the massacre he had witnessed here, he planned to track down the band of marauders and find Murphy, the man who had engineered this slaughter.

Cody's hands had closed around the saddle horn and he had lifted his foot into the stirrup when he heard the first muffled scream. His eyes swept fervently over the plain, seeing no sign of life. Then he heard a rapid thumping. His eyes darted to the Rutheford wagon. The sound came from there. He rushed to the blazing prairie schooner. He knew many emigrants had secret compartments built into their wagons, usually for hiding valuables, and it made sense Carl Rutheford would have one for his Jenny.

The screams emanating from the wagon box became more panic stricken. Cody scoured the ground for anything he could use to break open the box. He snatched a crowbar from the grass and sprinted to the wagon. Clutching the lever in his fists, he drove the flattened end between two boards and pushed against it with all his might. The intense heat of the flames scorched his face and the back's of his hands as he leaned into the bar. Finally, with the deep squawk of nails being rent from lumber, one of the boards gave way.

A pair of hands came into view, shoving against the loosened board.

Cody hammered the steel bar into the wagon box again, in an attempt to widen the break. The second plank splintered and Jenny Rutheford lunged through the gap. The hem of her dress caught fire as she came through the breach and knocked Cody to the ground.

Jenny staggered to her feet, but Bailey, seeing the flames on the back of her dress, grabbed her around the waist and threw her to the ground. He rolled her back and forth over the sandy soil as she screamed for him to get off.

"Hold still! You were on fire!"

She ceased her resistance.

"It's all out now," Cody said as he stood and offered Jenny his hand.

She looked up, realizing for the first time who her rescuer was.

"Cody? Oh, Cody," she cried as she threw her arms around his neck. "I thought I was going to be burned alive."

"You almost were," he said, embracing her awkwardly.

She pulled away from him, wiping her tears away with her fingers.

"I heard gunshots," she said, sniffling hard. "And screams."

Cody reached out and took her by the shoulders, turning her back to the corpse-littered basin.

"We need to get away from these wagons."

She struggled to free herself from his grip.

"I've got to find my mama and papa," she protested.

"Jenny, I'm sorry," he said, shaking his head.

"Sorry? For what? Let me go!"

"All right, I will, but just hold on a minute. You've got to listen to me. Your pa took care to see that you had a safe place to hide when trouble came. Well, bad trouble did, Jenny, and you're the only one to survive it."

Her eyes widened. "No. I don't believe you."

"It's the truth. I'm gonna let you go and you're gonna see some mighty ugly things. Folks've been killed and scalped."

She spun away from him and beheld the mutilated bodies of her parents. Cody stood ready to catch her if she fainted, but she stood firm.

"Is this what happened to everyone?"

"Near as I can tell."

Jenny began walking among the mangled bodies, shaking her head and gasping.

Bailey stayed close beside her, waiting for her to collapse once her initial shock had passed, but she didn't waver as she made her grim journey.

"How could they do this? I never supposed all of the stories about Indian cruelties were true, but—" She bit her lip as the tears rose in her eyes.

"It wasn't Indians, Jenny. It was Murphy."

"Murphy? How do you know that?"

"It's a long tale and I'll tell it as soon as we get away from here."

"We've got to see to the burying," she said, a faraway look in her eyes.

Cody's eyes swept over the basin. They didn't have time to bury one person and he counted at least twenty bodies.

"We don't have time for that, Jenny."

She wheeled on him. "What do you want to do? Leave them for the wild animals? They have to be covered."

"Look, when Murphy and his men get together and cover what happened here, that pilot's gonna be askin' for an accountin'. Look around you. What do you think will happen when they realize you weren't numbered among the dead? I'll tell you what, they'll be comin' back for you."

# CHAPTER 10

JENNY bit her lower lip, fighting back the tears. "I can't just leave my mama and papa laying here. Can't we at least bury them?"

Cody emitted a heavy sigh. He wanted to tell her yes, but knew he couldn't.

"We don't know how far away them boys had to ride to meet up with Murphy," he said. "And I don't think your folks would want you to risk your life buryin' them. They're beyond carin' about that kind of thing."

Her eyes searched the prairie around her, until she spotted a broken-handled shovel. With resolute steps she stalked through the grass and picked up the implement. She grasped it in her hands, holding it across her body like a musket.

"Are you going to find one to help me?" she asked defiantly.

Cody pushed his hat back on his head. Though he felt sorry for her loss, he considered her stubbornness foolish. She didn't seem to realize the danger that threatened them. He did, however, and decided to have nothing to do with the nonsense she proposed. Cody wheeled toward Champion and swung onto the pinto's back. He spurred the horse forward to where Jenny clutched her broken shovel, then halted. He held out his left hand to her.

"You won't help me?"

"We can't stay here another minute," he said softly. "Come with me now and there's a good chance we can see that Murphy pays for this. But if we keep hangin' around here, we're gonna wind up dead for sure."

Her cheeks flushed and her eyes stared at him coldly.

"I understand," she said hostilely. "You're scared."

"Look, I figure them renegades outnumber us ten to one. Me, they'll probably kill outright. But you? You're a fine-lookin' young woman and I reckon they won't be in such a hurry to be rid of you."

"You're just saying that to frighten me," she said, but the anger in her voice had lost its forcefulness.

"Maybe I am." He offered his hand to her again. "But I remember the look in your eyes that day in Wilkes's store when Murphy was lookin' at you through the window. You think about that and you'll know I ain't just trying to scare you, I'm trying to save you."

She blinked her eyes rapidly and the tears began to flow down her cheeks. The shovel slipped from her grasp and dropped to the ground. She reached for Cody's hand and he pulled her up behind him.

"Hold onto me tight," Cody ordered. "We're gonna be doin' some hard ridin'."

The Pony rider spurred Champion sharply as he turned him back toward the river, and the gelding lurched into a gallop. Cody felt Jenny's arms encircle his waist as Champion began his flight across the prairie.

Jenny looked back at the inferno she had escaped and laid her head against Cody's back, letting the tears flow freely. Her heart beat heavily in her chest, weighted with self-reproach. How many times had she allowed anger at her parents to come between them? She had resorted to self-indulgent pouting to punish them for taking her away from her home and friends. Only this morning she had behaved sullenly with her mother, refusing to help with the unloading of the Franklins' wagon. And then her mother had come to the wagon, her eyes wide and her face white with fear. She had ushered Jenny into the narrow, coffinlike hideout, kissing her daughter and brushing wisps of blonde hair from her face as tears streamed down her cheeks. She had told her mother that she loved her, but she had never gotten the opportunity to tell her father. The burden of her grief choked her, causing her to gasp for breath. Her arms tightened about Cody's waist as she wept.

As they rode on the open prairie, Cody wondered if Murphy's bunch had any good trackers among them. As former Comancheros they might even have an Indian or two riding with them. Cody had learned some about reading sign from old Pop, enough to know the trail they were now laying down on the prairie wouldn't be hard for an experienced tracker to follow. Of course if they suspected Cody had come upon the train, then no tracker would be needed—the wild bunch would head for the next Pony station at Freemont Springs.

Ike Pappas spurred his horse ahead as he lead the rest of the men toward the rendezvous. He wanted to reach Murphy first and try and explain why they didn't have the girl. The raid had gone badly from the moment they had attacked the emigrant train. The pilgrims had fought better than Murphy had led him to believe they were capable of. Then on top of that, some of the men had become overly eager and torched the wagons before anyone had sufficient opportunity to search them. If those wagons had held any gold it now lay melted among ashes too hot to sift through. When the men had realized how little money the emigrants had, they had turned mean and bloodthirsty, more than willing to carry out Murphy's orders to murder. The bloodletting didn't phase Ike. He had seen too much of that before. However, he couldn't recall any time when he had heard so much grumbling against Big Joe, even though some of these men had ridden with him for years. Several had asked Ike why Murphy had chosen such an obviously poor train, but he hadn't answered, even though he had expected a young blonde girl had influenced Murphy's decision.

Big Joe squatted on his haunches, chewing his quid and scratching in the dirt with the tip of his bowie as Ike galloped into camp. Murphy grunted as he slowly rose to his feet.

"Where's ever'body?"

"Comin' along," Ike said, hitching his thumb over his shoulder. "I rode on ahead."

Murphy spat into the dust. "Why'd you leave the girl with 'em?"

Ike swung off his horse, dropping to the ground in front of Big Joe. "There warn't no gal, Joe."

The pilot's nostrils flared as he sucked in a deep breath.

"What do ya mean?" He grabbed the lapels of Ike's vest in his fists. "Did ya foul it all up, Ike?"

Grabbing hold of Murphy's wrists, Ike tried to wriggle from Murphy's grasp.

"I never saw her, Big Joe! I swear, I looked high and low and never saw no sign of her!"

Murphy stared hard into Ike's eyes, then finally gave him a violent shove, almost landing Ike on the ground. Pappas straightened his clothing, his eyes riveted on Murphy.

"Somethin' else ya better know."

"What's that?" Murphy growled.

"We had mighty poor pickin's."

"So what?" he said, waving Ike away. "We've had bad hauls before."

"Yeah, but you built this one up to be somethin' special."

Big Joe had stopped listening, his mind filled with the mystery of the missing emigrant girl. He had seen her this very morning when she had eaten breakfast with her family. Where had she hidden? Then it came to him.

"You check them schooners for hideouts?"

Ike swallowed hard as the nerve beneath his right eye

began twitching. He had expected this question before now, but still had no more of an answer than when he had first ridden into Big Joe's camp.

"Some of the boys got carried away and torched the wagons before we got the chance to look 'em over."

Big Joe squeezed his eyes shut. Then suddenly they flew open as he hurled a hammer blow that landed on Ike's left cheekbone, splitting the skin wide open. The impact of the punch lifted Pappas off his feet and dropped him to the ground.

"What's the matter with you?" Murphy bellowed. "Ain't you strong enough to keep discipline anymore?"

Ike propped himself up on one elbow, gingerly touching his cheek with his gloved fingertips. He drew his hand back and studied the blood on his glove, then untied the bandanna around his neck and pressed it against the wound before lifting his eyes to Murphy. He started to reply, but the sound of approaching hoofbeats stopped him.

"Them boys ridin' in here ain't much richer than the last time you seen 'em. They're gonna want to know what happened to all that loot ya promised 'em. Especially after they killed ever'body like ya said."

"Hmmph! So ya followed *that* order, huh?"

Murphy extended his hand to Ike and helped him to his feet. They both faced the incoming riders.

"Well, Ike tells me you boys got a mite carried away!" Big Joe shouted as the men reined their horses to a halt.

"That wasn't no rich emigrant train," said a voice from the midst of the settling dust.

A few others grumbled in agreement.

Murphy stared at each face, taking his time to study every pair of eyes. After a long, heavy silence he finally spoke again.

"Who put them wagons to the torch before anybody had a chance to rifle through 'em? Huh? Somebody better speak up, 'cause I wanna know which one o' you idiots ruined it for ever'body!"

No one spoke.

"Well, at least ya got enough gumption not to sell each other out. But ya shore knotted things up. Didn't it occur to any o' you fire-happy squareheads that the gold was in them wagons?"

"There wasn't no gold," one of the men said, spurring his horse forward. "That was just a buncha dirt poor pilgrims. Admit it. You just loused it—"

The Walker Colt appeared in Murphy's hand and belched fire and lead. The bandit lurched from his saddle into the dirt. Murphy cocked the revolver again.

"Now," he said with a humorless smile appearing from within the thick brush that covered the lower half of his face. "Is there anybody else who wants to blame me for their own stupidity?"

A few of the men exchanged uneasy glances, but no one spoke.

"Good." Murphy holstered his gun.

"I understand from Ike here that our count of the dead don't match," he lied. "Seems while you firebugs were torchin' ever'thing in sight, one of them emigrants escaped. So, not only did ya lose the gold, ya also managed to leave somebody alive that can identify us."

"What've ya got in mind to do, Big Joe?" Ike asked.

"Ain't much we can do 'cept go back and see if we can track 'em down."

A murmur arose from the ranks. No strangers to violence, these men had joined Murphy's band for the promise of easy wealth and hadn't flinched when the means to reach that end had included murder. They had wiped out emigrant trains before, including women and small children. This time they had made no effort to disguise themselves and knew the dreadful consequences if that lone emigrant survived.

"The blood of them pilgrims is on ever'body's hands," Murphy said, sensing their thoughts. "One of us does the strangulation jig, we all do."

Ike bent over and retrieved his hat, brushing the dust from its crown before slapping it on his head.

"Reckon it'll take all of us?" he asked.

Murphy scratched his hard jaw through his beard. "I s'pose ever'body oughta go. Many hands make light work, eh?"

No one spoke as Ike mounted up.

Murphy stepped into the stirrup and swung into the saddle of the tall roan. His eyes roved from one face to another, searching for the turncoats in his midst. He knew they were there; they always were whenever things didn't go according to plan, and sometimes even when they did. He had already killed one and had no doubt others would follow. He yanked the reins, turning his horse southeastward, and started back toward the emigrant train.

The rest of the men fell dutifully in behind him. A few of them still believed in Big Joe and his promises, remembering times when he had brought emigrant trains rich with loot into their web, but their numbers were dwindling and almost all of the men had come to look upon Ike as their leader. Whenever Murphy disappeared for weeks at a time to ferret out the next victims Ike became their commander, and they considered him one of their own, unlike Big Joe, whom they viewed as a harsh taskmaster. They feared Murphy, although loath to admit it. He stood more than a head taller than any of them and the scars around his eyes and on his knuckles gave mute testimony to his violent nature. He didn't tolerate dissent from anyone, not even Ike, who had ridden with him since before the days of the forty-niners, and any man who dared to cross him usually ended up dead.

The procession of cutthroats snaked over the prairie, a

long dark line of deadly poison ready to strike the emigrant who threatened them.

"What're ya gonna tell ever'body about this girl, Big Joe?" Ike asked as he and Murphy rode ahead of the others.

"What's to tell?"

"If it wasn't the girl that escaped, would we still be makin' this ride?"

"What do you think?" Murphy asked gruffly.

Ike didn't respond.

"Well, Chester finally got back," Murphy said as he leaned in his saddle toward Ike.

"Whar is he? What happened?"

"Hmmph! He's layin' dead back there," Murphy said, pointing over his shoulder. "He said they took care of that trooper and whatever he knew he took with him to his grave."

"What about Woody and the rest of 'em?"

"Dead, too."

"That soldier boy killed 'em all?"

Murphy shrugged.

"Chester wasn't able to say too much. He was on his last leg by the time he got here. But he said they took care of him. So all we gotta worry about now is that poor little emigrant girl."

# CHAPTER 11

JOHN Butler and Everett Samuels galloped into the yard at Freemont Springs, their horses blowing and lathered. The station had a few more amenities than Cold Springs. Two huts connected by a roof of thatched timber served as headquarters, with a lean-to stable next to a flimsy pole and rope corral.

The riders brought the horses to an abrupt halt and both men swung out of their saddles. John tossed the reins of the palomino to Everett.

"See to the horses! I'll check on Cody!"

Everett led the weary animals to the corral, then stripped off their saddles and blankets and began rubbing them down.

Crig Rogers, the head stockman, bolted through the door of the station's headquarters, meeting John in the yard.

"Where's Cody?" Rogers asked.

A dark frown creased John's forehead as he swept his black hat with its wide brim and flat crown from his head. "I was hopin' you could tell me."

"Reckon that means you ain't got the mail either?" John shook his head. "That's what it means."

Crig scratched the end of his nose as he shook his head. "I never knowed Cody to be so late."

"Well, that ain't the only mystery."

"What d'ya mean?"

"The station at Cold Springs has been wiped out."

Crig's pointed chin dropped.

"You mean ever'body's dead?"

John nodded, then relayed the story of Bob Lassiter's arrival at Bonner's station and of the subsequent discoveries at Cold Springs.

Crig shook his head in amazement. "Think it was Injuns?"

"No sign it was."

"I'll be. You boys want some coffee? It ain't fresh, but it's hot."

"We're gonna need fresh mounts," Everett said as he shuffled toward John and Crig. "Them two are nearly played out."

"Boz's gone into town, but I'm sure he won't object to swapping a couple horses with you. If I was you, I'd take that gray and that buckskin, they're stayers."

Everett gave Crig a mock salute as he started back to the corral.

"How 'bout that coffee?"

"No thanks," John replied. "We'll just fill our canteens and be on our way. Are you gonna be all right here?"

A toothy smile spread over Crig's face.

"There's me an' Josh Carpenter. We'll be fine till Boz and Emory get back."

"We'll be on our way, then." He spun on his heel and strode across the yard, while Crig disappeared inside one of the huts.

Everett had already thrown John's saddle on the buckskin and stood beside the gray, tightening the cinch on his own saddle. John collected their canteens, slinging them over his shoulder as he scurried to the trough near the stable, where he began filling the containers.

Crig emerged from the headquarters structure, carrying a pair of saddlebags. He hauled them to the corral and handed them to Everett, who had mounted the gray.

"Got some fried sage hen in there and a coupla boiled eggs. Thought you fellas might get hungry out there huntin' Cody."

"Thanks, Crig," Everett said as he secured the saddle-bags behind the cantle.

John returned from the trough and tossed Everett his canteen, then climbed aboard the buckskin.

The Freemont Springs stockman opened the Texas gate.

"You fellas stay sharp!" Crig called.

"We'll be seein' you," John said, waving with his hat as he wheeled his horse through the gate. Then he slapped the buckskin's flank with his hat and the steed lunged for the prairie. Everett and the gray hit the breeze right behind him.

They pointed the horses eastward, heading back toward Cold Springs. The two rode about a half mile apart, one on either side of the Pony route, figuring they had a better chance of spotting Cody if he had gone down. It hadn't yet occurred to either man that Cody might have left the trail. At the halfway point between Freemont Springs and Cold Springs, John signaled Everett to join him.

"I don't get it," John said, arching his back as he sat astride his horse. "We ain't seen hide nor hair of Bailey, and it's beginning to make me feel as weary as a lame buffalo calf runnin' with a wolf pack."

Everett dug into the saddlebags Crig Rogers had given him and produced two pieces of fried prairie chicken. He offered one to John, who took it and gnawed it hungrily.

"Looks like that fire south of here has just about petered out," Everett observed, his cheek bulging like a chipmunk's. He pointed with the chicken leg. "Maybe Cody saw it and went scoutin'."

Turning in his saddle, Butler gazed over his right shoulder into the southwestern sky. They had seen a pillar of smoke climbing above the prairie as they had raced to Freemont Springs. They hadn't given it much thought at the time, consumed as they were with getting to the next relay station. But now Butler turned his attention on the column, which had spread at its peak until it now assumed the shape of a funnel.

John pushed his hat back on his head, then pulled at his earlobe as he studied the shadowy haze that hovered above the plains.

"That's a curiosity, but I don't know that it would have sidetracked Cody from his ride. He's one of them Pony riders that takes his oath to deliver the mail as something holy."

"Reckon that's so," Everett said. "But where else do we have to look for him?"

"All right," John said, as he brought the buckskin around. "Let's ride on over there nice and easy and have us a look."

John and Everett spurred the horses to a canter, heading for the river. They crossed the gray ribbon, journeying through the tall grass that billowed like the rolling waters of the deep. The sun burned hot upon the desert, and sweat oozed from their pores in the sweltering heat.

Everett tugged the blue cotton bandanna from around his neck and mopped his face.

"Man, it's shapin' up to be a scorcher."

"Won't hear any argument from me about that," John said, reaching for his canteen. He pulled the stopper with his teeth, then tipped the flask to his lips for a short sip of the brackish water. He wrinkled his nose in disgust. "Water don't keep long either."

He caught the plug in his teeth again and worked it back into the mouth of the canteen.

Suddenly they topped a rise and found themselves staring into the shallow basin where the charred, smoldering skeleton of the emigrant train rested with a flock of buzzards circling above it. The bodies of the victims lay concealed in the grass, a grotesque surprise waiting for the two stockmen. They urged their horses down the ridge, then goaded them into a lope.

John spotted the first mangled corpse as they reached the basin. "Oh, my lord!"

"What?"

"Take a look over here."

Everett guided the gray alongside John's horse, catching his breath sharply as his eyes beheld the mutilated body.

Big Joe and his men came upon the basin about twenty minutes after John and Everett, from the opposite direction. Ike spied the two men first and pointed them out to Murphy.

"We got company down there, Big Joe," Ike said.

"That's all right. I don't want no trouble with them two galoots. You can't be sure somebody else don't know they're out here. Pass the word along to the rest of the boys, and tell 'em we come from Julesburg, chasin' a band of renegades."

John saw the advancing procession first.

"Everett," he called, hardly raising his voice in the deadly silence of the basin.

His companion looked up from the opposite side of the hollow, then followed John's nod and spied the twisting serpent descending a low hill to the west. Immediately apprehensive, Everett moved across the depression to John's side.

"I don't think I like the look of this."

John bobbed his head in agreement.

"Yeah, somethin' ain't right. They don't look to be army, and who else would be ridin' out here in such a large bunch?"

They exchanged uneasy glances as the riders continued their approach.

"Well, it's too late to run," John observed. "We'll just have to try and dodge trouble if it comes."

He and Everett checked the loads in their pistols as

Murphy's pack neared the decimated train, then stood shoulder to shoulder waiting for the company to arrive.

"Howdy, fellas!" Murphy called from atop the roan. "Are you all that's left of this bunch?"

John shook his head as he inspected the rough string of men behind Big Joe. "We weren't part of this train. We spotted the smoke when we's ridin' a few miles north of here lookin' for a friend of ours. We came down to see if he followed it, but it don't appear that he did."

Murphy let his eyes drink in the mayhem he had ordered. His men had done a thorough job, except for the Rutheford girl. Bodies lay scattered throughout the rippling grass, along with the battered remnants of their possessions. Not one of the prairie schooners remained intact, almost all of them reduced to cinders.

"Yeah, it was that smoke that brung us over here, too. We come outa Julesburg nigh on to a week ago, trackin' a band of renegade Cheyenne. Reckon they musta hit these pilgrims."

Butler glanced at Everett and saw that his friend was studying the big man on the roan intently. John looked at Murphy and saw that he had also observed Everett's stare and didn't appear to like it.

"I know you, boy?" Big Joe inquired, arching his left eyebrow.

Everett shook his head slowly. "No, sir. I don't think so."

"Hmmph!" Murphy turned in his saddle. "Charillo! Take a coupla men and see if ya can find any sign of them Cheyenne!"

"Sí, Big Joe," a sinewy Indian responded, breaking from the ranks. Two other men followed.

"As soon as our tracker picks up the trail of them Injuns we'll be on our way."

"Could you spare a few men to help us bury these folks?" Everett asked.

Murphy guffawed. "Boy, we're chasin' down murderin'

Injuns. We ain't got time for no grave diggin'. Besides, these pilgrims're beyond helpin'. We'll be doin' them a bigger service by trackin' down the vermin that done this. Y'all are welcome to ride with us."

John shook his head. "No, we still have our friend to find."

"Suit yerselves, but you're takin' a mighty big chance, just the two of ya wanderin' out here alone."

"There's others searchin' besides us," Everett said casually.

Murphy nodded, but his eyes had left the two stockmen as he caught Charillo's signal.

"Looks like our tracker's found their sign," Big Joe said, turning his gaze back to John and Everett. "You fellas watch yer step. There's dangerous heathen about."

"Yes, sir, we'll do that," John responded as the others followed after the roan to where the Indian waited.

"What've ya got?" Murphy asked, keeping his voice low.

"One rider come from there," Charillo said, extending his arm as he pointed northeast. "His tracks mill around a bit before he dismounts. Then joined by others. Smaller. A woman I think."

"What?" Murphy seethed. "A woman? Are you sure?"

"Not sure, but I think so."

A smile tugged at the corner of Ike's mouth as he listened to the exchange.

Murphy turned in his saddle, his eyes sweeping the horsemen gathered behind him.

"Anybody that didn't hear what Charillo found?"

Blank stares met his inquiring eyes. He grunted in disgust and swung around.

"Have ya got anythin' else?"

"Sí, sí. The two mounted one horse and headed west, moving toward the river."

Big Joe nodded.

"Can ya tell how long ago?"

"Maybe a couple hours."

"All right, then. Let's get goin'."

"They got a pretty good jump on us," Ike said quietly, so only Murphy could hear him. "Our horses are gettin' done in. They've covered a powerful lot o' ground this mornin'."

Murphy's left eyebrow shot up. "Well, what d'ya wanna do, Ike? Forget about 'em?"

"They might've already reached help, Big Joe. We could be headin' right into a hornet's nest."

The pilot stroked his beard thoughtfully.

"Ain't nothin' north out here but stage relays and the Pony Express stations. And if they're ridin' double they ain't gonna make very good time. Nope. I'd say we got 'em nearly roped in."

Ike shrugged.

"Then let's get after 'em."

John and Everett watched as the outlaw band wheeled their horses northward and thundered away from the emigrant train.

"Whew!" John sighed. "Can't say I'm sorry to see them go."

"Me, either," Everett agreed.

"What about that big fella ridin' the roan? Did you know him?"

"I don't think so."

"Well, one thing I can tell you, this wasn't no Indian attack. Why, I ain't even found a single arrowhead, or a feather. And I got a feelin' them boys weren't from Julesburg either."

"Why's that?"

John pushed his wide-brimmed hat back on his head as he gazed after the retreating band of horsemen. "Just a notion I got. Let's go have a look at what their tracker found."

# CHAPTER 12

"CAN'T we go any faster?" Jenny demanded.

"Champ's been on the run since dawn. Probably got more than twenty miles behind him already."

"Well, he's a horse. Aren't they made for running with people on their backs?"

Cody shook his head. He had run Champion for nearly two miles right after they had left the train, but even the hardy mustang couldn't keep up such a punishing pace for very long. And if Murphy and his men caught them afoot, well, that would be the end of it. So he had slowed the pinto to a trot for about a mile, then finally reined him to a walk in an effort to conserve the pinto's energy. He had kept an uneasy eye on the skyline behind them, expecting at any moment to see the dust of Murphy's pirates hanging over the horizon.

The Pony rider had another concern as well. The late morning sun had heated the plains like a stove top, and Cody knew such mugginess spawned savage thunderstorms that struck with the quickness of a prairie wildfire and whose black clouds convulsed across the sky like the smoke of that calamity of nature. They hit suddenly and ferociously, drenching the desert, jarring the land with booming thunder and searing it with the white heat of lightning. He had no desire to face such an ordeal out here in the open with Jenny.

Under other circumstances he would have enjoyed the thought of sharing his poncho in the rain with the beautiful emigrant girl. Jenny's anger toward him, he understood, was her way of dealing with the tragedy she had endured. She had lost everything except her own life back there in that basin. She had seen the death her parents had suffered—not a quiet passing while some preacher held their hands, but a brutal slaughter. And he had stopped her from laying them to rest.

An ominous rumbling in the west drew him out of his thoughts.

"What was that?" Jenny asked.

Cody studied the darkening western sky, his apprehension increasing. "We could be in for some rain."

"Like the rain we had the other day in that town of yours?"

He nodded. "Maybe worse."

He estimated the station at Freemont Springs still lay more than two hours away if they maintained their present pace and he had no intention of hurrying now. Champion needed the rest and Cody wanted him to have it. If that meant riding out a storm, then that is what they would do.

Cody reined the mustang to a halt when he felt the first sprinkles and dismounted, swinging his right leg over the horse's neck and dropping to the ground. He held out his arms to Jenny.

"I know how to get off a horse, thank you," she said scornfully.

Cody backed away and let her climb down.

"Why are we stopping here?"

"I got an oilskin poncho in that roll behind the cantle, thought maybe you'd like to wear it. It'll keep you pretty dry."

Jenny stared into his blue eyes. He had saved her life twice, rescuing her from that burning coffin of a wagon, then taking her with him when it would probably have been easier to have left her. But Cody had made her leave her father and mother lying back there on the prairie for the wild beasts to prey upon and she found it hard to forgive him of that.

She spun away from him, then left the horse's side so Cody could untie the strings holding the blanket roll on the saddle. More raindrops began falling as he spread the blanket on the ground, exposing the poncho rolled inside.

"Here you are," he said, extending the garment to her. "You just slip your head through that hole in the center, then it just drapes over you."

"Thank you," Jenny said softly as she took the poncho from him.

"You might want to pull it up over your head and just look out through the hole. Might keep you drier."

The couple had hardly settled onto Champion's back before the downpour commenced. Cody pulled his hat down tight on his head, then took the reins and gently spurred the gelding. As the horse began plodding through the drenching rain, it occurred to Cody the storm would wash out the trail they had left, perhaps buying them time to put more distance between themselves and the outlaws behind them. That Murphy and his men followed, the Pony rider had no doubt. As soon as the pilot realized Jenny had survived, they would be coming for her—they didn't dare let her live.

"Will you be able to find your way in this rain?" she asked.

He smiled, no longer detecting animosity in her voice.

"If we get lost, we head due north until we come to the river, then turn left. Don't worry, I'll get us there in one piece. We might be soaked to the bone, but we'll be in one piece."

"Cody?"

"Yeah?"

"I'm sorry for treating you so badly. You saved my life and I've behaved terribly toward you."

Jenny laid her head against his back as her arms encircled his waist, clasping her hands over his firm stomach. He gently stroked her hands.

"I was sure you hated me," he said.

"I guess I thought I did. It's just that it was so hard to leave my mother and father that way." Her voice broke.

"That's all right. I understand."

Jenny's loss made him recollect the death of his own parents, victims of the war between the free state and pro-slavery factions along the border between Missouri and the newly admitted state of Kansas. He knew too well the wrenching pain and terrible hollowness wrought by the violence people unleashed upon one another. It had robbed him of his family too. And it would rob them of their lives if they didn't reach Freemont Springs before Murphy caught up with them.

The rain fell in sheets so dense that Cody's eyes began to ache from peering into the soaking, gray barrage. The spate had almost flattened the brim of his hat against the back of his neck and forehead and had plastered his cotton shirt to his body. As much as Cody detested this sousing, he knew the unpredictable weather played its role in contributing to the volatile nature of this land, and if the sun returned to its perch today it meant a suffocatingly torrid afternoon. The Pony rider didn't relish the thought of riding double beneath the scorching sun, but accepted they had no choice if the storm broke before they reached the next relay station.

Charillo squatted, inspecting the ground. The tracks had vanished in the rain. He stood, holding the reins of his horse clasped in both hands, still staring at the washed-out trail, seeing nothing.

"Well, what've ya got?" Murphy demanded from atop the roan.

The Indian's face betrayed no emotion as he gazed at Murphy, water running off the brim of his hat.

"Tracks gone."

"Gone?"

"Sí. The rain."

"I was afraid this'd happen, Big Joe," Ike said through clenched teeth.

"Shut up," Murphy snarled. He focused his attention on the tracker. "What d'ya think?"

"Tracks point northwest long time," he replied as he pointed into the storm.

The outlaw leader stared past Charillo's crooked finger. "What lies in that direction?"

"The river," Ike said. "The stage road, relay stations. People."

"Ya got somethin' ya wanna say, Ike, say it!" Murphy growled.

"Seems to me we're headed for trouble if we don't let this go. Let's just turn around and head for Texas. Forget that girl of yours."

The blood rushed into the pilot's wide face as he stared bug-eyed at Ike.

"I ain't the one that let this girl get away!" he shouted. "And it wasn't me that burned up the wagons 'fore anybody got to check 'em! You was in charge of that part of the plan and ya botched it! She musta seen you and the rest of the boys, and now you're whinin' at me 'cause I'm tryin' to clean up the mess you've made of everythin'! What's it gonna be, Ike? Ya gonna turn tail and run, or ya gonna help the rest of us do what we gotta do?"

Ike's eyes locked with Murphy's and held them for a moment before breaking off and scanning the faces of the men who stared grimly at him through the downpour. "I'm in."

"Good," Murphy grunted with a nod. "Charillo, get on yer horse. We're headin' northwest."

Ike lagged behind, watching the others file in front of him as they rode after Big Joe in a disjointed column. He had always followed Murphy. And since the early days in Texas he had never questioned the bandit leader, or tried to second-guess his intentions. This business with the emigrant girl, however, was changing that. He had never seen Murphy so obsessed with anything, let alone a woman, and the daughter of some emigrant at that. But Ike had also ridden with Murphy long enough to know you didn't challenge him with others looking on, for then he became meaner than a hungry wolf, killing without hesitation.

Ike piloted his horse to fall in and bring up the rear of Murphy's troop. If an ambush lay ahead, he had a better chance for survival if he rode at the tail end of the procession. He could also keep an eye on their backtrail.

Big Joe turned in his saddle as the roan plodded after Charillo and fished a plug of tobacco from his saddlebags. He reached inside his slicker and withdrew his bowie from the wide leather belt that girded his waist, then cut a chaw, and fed it into his mouth. He returned the knife to its sheath, then tugged the slicker closed, chewing his cud and wishing he had a bottle of whiskey to burn off the chill from the rain.

He dug his heels into the roan and the horse trotted toward Charillo, who rode fifty yards ahead. The Indian didn't even look up as he approached, and that annoyed Murphy. Charillo never exhibited the deference the rest of the band showed him, and that rankled the outlaw leader, even though he knew most of the men feigned their respect. However, the Comanche tracker didn't openly rebel against Big Joe's authority and that, plus his abilities reading sign, made it easier for Murphy to tolerate him.

"See anythin'?"

Charillo lifted his wide face to the sky as he shook his head.

"Too much rain," he replied, letting the water run down

over his flat cheekbones. He faced Murphy. "We won't find any more tracks."

The pilot grunted, conveying his disgust.

"How much time we take to find this white girl?" Charillo asked.

"Why? You gettin' like old Ike?"

"Pappas knows much trouble comes."

Big Joe squinted at the stoic Comanche beside him. "If ya know somethin' let's hear it. Otherwise, hobble yer lip. I'm beginnin' to think I'm surrounded by a bunch of women."

The outlaw's remark didn't phase Charillo.

A silence fell between them.

For the first time Murphy wondered if he had made the right decision in pursuing the Rutheford girl. If he rode into the first settlement he came to and fabricated a story about returning to the train and finding it decimated, he could establish an alibi. Obviously the girl hadn't seen much of the attack, or Ike would have captured her. Of course, there were those two men they had met earlier, but a way could be found to deal with them.

Then he thought about Jenny, her honey-colored hair, the soft lines of her oval face and the smooth contours of her young body. He had to have her. He had come too far and risked too much to turn his back on this chance.

He had intentionally misled everyone, including Ike. He had known from the start, when he had met the Rutheford train in Independence, that they had carried no great wealth. Most everyone in the caravan had left poor dirt farms behind, hoping to find better in the west, except for Carl Rutheford. Murphy had suspected Rutheford carried a full purse, though not enough to make it worthwhile for the whole gang of cutthroats to take on the emigrants. The only reason he had devised the attack was to get Jenny Rutheford.

Murphy halted his horse and spat into the mud, letting

Charillo take the point alone. He chewed leisurely, scratching his square jaw through his black and gray beard as he waited for the column to catch up. His eyes narrowed as they approached and he realized Ike didn't hold the lead position. He spurred his horse to a swift trot alongside the ragged line, searching for Ike, finally spying him at the rear. Murphy let Ike ride past him, then turned the roan to come up beside Ike.

"What're ya doin' back here?" Big Joe inquired without a hint of rancor in his voice.

"Keepin' an eye on our backside. What does it look like?"

Murphy noted the insolence in Ike's tone. "Are ya ready to have it out with me, Ike?" he demanded, keeping his voice low.

Ike cocked his head, peering at Murphy from beneath the drooping brim of his hat. "Ya want me to ride up front? Just say so. I done followed ya on one of the most foolish ventures ever without questionin' yer orders, so why would I start now?"

"Speak plain, Pappas," Big Joe growled low like a wary hound.

"And get a bullet for my trouble? Thanks, but I don't think so."

Murphy sat back in his saddle as though Ike had struck him. He had no inclination to kill Ike. Sure, he got rough with Ike once in a while, but he had never pulled a gun on him, or threatened to kill him.

"Ya think I'd kill ya, Ike?"

The rawboned Texan snorted. "Seen ya do it often enough."

"Ride where ya will, Ike," he said, then goaded the roan to the head of the string.

# CHAPTER 13

JOHN and Everett poked among the grass, searching for the telltale sign that had sent the band of riders heading northwest. Everett found it first.

"Over here, Johnny!"

"Find somethin'?"

"I'll say. And I don't like the look of it none either," Everett said, squatting on his haunches. John hunkered down beside him.

"Take a look at this shoe print," he said, carefully folding the grass back from the indentation in the dirt. "If you look at the right corner you can see a notch has been filed on the inside edge."

"I see it."

"Well, every horse at Bonner's has that notch on the shoe of the left hind foot."

"I'd forgotten about that. Silas ordered it, didn't he?"

"One of my first jobs was notchin' them shoes. Silas wanted to make it easier to track our horses, case Indians decided to make off with 'em."

"Or outlaws," John said, lifting his eyes to the horizon where he had last seen Murphy's riders.

"I got no doubts this is Champion's shoe, but it looks like he's carryin' more of a load than Cody and the mail."

John furrowed his brow and stood. "Meanin' maybe Cody picked somebody up here."

"Looks like it," Everett said, rising.

"Wonder what that has to do with them fellows from Julesburg?"

"Thought you said you didn't believe they were from Julesburg?"

John smiled. "I don't. Does it make sense to you for fifteen or twenty able-bodied men to ride nearly a hundred miles huntin' Indians? Leaving their homes and businesses unprotected?"

"Would be kinda stupid."

"Hmmph! Stupid, all right. And that fella that led them boys in here looked a lot more mean than he did stupid."

John loosened the knot in the bandanna around his neck and snapped it off. He removed his flat-crowned hat and wiped the sweatband, then mopped the sweat from his face with the kerchief.

"I got a feelin' them boys came here lookin' for somethin' or someone in particular," John said, settling the hat on his head.

"I expect Cody's in trouble."

"I'd bet the farm them fellas that rode outa here are after him. And it wouldn't surprise me none if they didn't have somethin' to do with whatever happened back yonder at Cold Springs."

"Then we best be on our way."

The two started for their horses, the tall grass swishing against their legs. They climbed into their saddles and wheeled the gray and the buckskin north.

"You can bet Cody's on his way to Freemont Springs," John said as he pulled his hat down tight. "And that gives us an advantage if that other bunch is trackin' him. They'll be movin' a lot slower, tryin' to read his sign."

"Stands to reason they would. And I expect if we run into them again we'll end up with the grass wavin' over us."

"I hope Cody's makin' a straight-cut for the Pony station. That Champ's the toughest mustang I've ever seen, but he's got to be wearin' down."

As John kicked the buckskin to a gallop he twisted in his

saddle, shouting to Everett. "Stay off the skyline! I don't wanna risk bein' seen!"

Everett gave him a wave as his horse bounded after the buckskin.

The midafternoon sun made no effort to show itself among the heavy gray clouds that wept over the prairie. Except for the steady drumming of the rain the plains had fallen silent, a vast emptiness, seemingly devoid of any life but that of the tenacious mustang and his equally determined riders.

Cody rubbed his eyes, then stared hard into the wall of water before him. He believed he had caught a glimpse of the Freemont Springs Pony Express Station in the distance, but he hadn't thought they were so close. He was studying the terrain in front of them again, ready to discount his previous sighting as nothing more than wishful thinking, when he spied the station house. This time he had no doubt about what he saw. He touched his spurs to Champion and the mustang picked up his pace.

"What is it?" Jenny asked.

"Freemont Springs, straight ahead."

"I knew you'd get us here."

"So did I. I was just wonderin' when."

A wave of relief washed over Cody as they entered the yard at Freemont Springs. He and Jenny had eluded Murphy's savages and reached the safety of the Pony depot. He looked forward to passing the mochila to one of the stockmen and getting out of the rain.

The door of the headquarters swung open and stationmaster Julius Bosworth, a short, thick-set man, stood framed in the doorway, a shock of carrot-colored hair hanging over his low forehead.

"It's me, Boz. Cody Bailey."

The shiny skin of Bosworth's already puffy face swelled even more as it stretched to accommodate a smile.

"Good to see you, boy! Climb off o' there and cool yer saddle. Hey!" he called over his shoulder. "Cody's in!"

Cody dropped to the muddy yard, then aided Jenny as she dismounted. He grasped her arm and guided her toward the entrance of the cabin on their left. They stepped into the low-ceilinged dwelling and Boz closed the door behind them.

Crig Rogers stood against the back wall, on the far side of a crude table where Emory Tatum and Josh Carpenter sat with a checkerboard between them. To the right of the entry, not two steps behind Carpenter, stood a small stove that did double duty for cooking and heating. Four bunks crowded the opposite end of the room, completing the furnishings. Two windows flanked the door, and four hats and oilskins hung on pegs between the door frame and the panes to Cody's right.

The three men grinned at Cody as he stood by the door with water dripping from his clothes into pools quickly forming at his feet.

"Been worried 'bout you, Cody boy," Boz wheezed.

"Ran into some trouble south of here."

Jenny lowered the poncho from her head, and for the first time, Boz realized she was a female.

"Well, you gotta be the prettiest package I've ever seen on the Pony." He turned to the checker players. "Ain't either one of you educated in the social graces?"

Josh and Emory exchanged puzzled looks.

"Let the lady have a chair!"

Both men scrambled to their feet, nearly spilling the checkers onto the dirt floor as they tendered their apologies.

"Here, darlin'," Boz cooed. "Let me help you off with that oilskin before you sit yerself down."

Jenny glanced nervously at Cody, who smiled and nodded at her.

"Gents, meet Miss Jenny Rutheford."

The men murmured their greetings and introductions.

"Can I get you a cup of coffee, miss?" Emory asked.

"Just water, if you don't mind," she said, seating herself at the table.

"Water?" Boz snorted. "Think you'd have had enough o' that. How 'bout you, Cody?"

"I'll take the coffee," he replied as he sat down across from Jenny, sweeping his waterlogged hat from his head and tossing it onto the tabletop.

"So, what's yer story, Bailey?" Boz asked.

Cody told them of his conversation with Pop McCready two days earlier in Parker's Junction and about Pop's death. He reported the massacre at Cold Springs, along with Captain Conway's declaration that Joe Murphy led a band of renegades. Finally, he related his discovery of the slaughter of the emigrants.

"I convinced Jenny to come here with me. I'd seen this Murphy fella and figured he wouldn't hesitate a lick to get to her if he thought she was alive."

"I was nearly burned alive and he saved my life. If Cody hadn't come along—" She choked back a sob.

Boz shook his head in disbelief. He said to Cody, "You think them varmints'll try to foller you?"

"I reckon they will."

"Did you ever run into Butler and Samuels?" Crig asked.

Cody swallowed hard as he shook his head.

"They come a-thunderin' in here this mornin' lookin' for you. When I told 'em you hadn't been through they doubled back to Cold Springs."

"Boz, can one of your boys take the mail on?"

"I'll take it," Josh Carpenter piped up. "If it's all right with you, Boz?"

"Get ya a horse. Emory, help him get mounted up."

The two men bolted across the room, hooking hats and slickers as they charged out the door.

"I better see to Champ," Cody said.

"They'll take care of him. You just sit there and dry out a bit," Boz ordered. "Besides that, we gotta figger out what we're gonna do if them rascals show up here."

"Well, I don't think we oughta just sit around here and wait on 'em," Cody said evenly. "If they got back to the wagon train before this storm hit I expect they'll be comin' along the same route me and Jenny took. And that means we ain't got much time before they get here."

"You think the rain wiped out yer trail?" Crig Rogers asked.

"Even if it did, that would mean they'd just take longer to get here." He gazed at Boz, then at Crig. He wanted them to understand the seriousness of this situation without frightening Jenny any more than necessary.

Boz nodded thoughtfully. "Maybe once Josh is off, I could send Emory on a scoutin' trip to the south."

"Sounds like I better bring in a powder keg and some extra shot," Crig said, heading for the door. He pulled on his oilskin coat, then plucked a floppy slouch hat from the row of pegs and set it on his head. He gave the brim a sharp tug before leaving the hut.

"What about John and Everett?" Cody asked.

The stationmaster shrugged. "I don't know no more than Crig already told you. I wasn't here when they came in this mornin'."

"Hmm. I'll bet you're hungry," Cody said to Jenny. "Don't reckon you've had anything since breakfast."

"I guess I am," she said, managing a weak smile.

"Let me rustle up some grub for you," Boz volunteered.

Cody studied her ashen face as Boz began banging around the cast iron stove in back of him. She had shown tremendous bravery today. Behind the weariness in her blue eyes he saw courage and determination.

"Are you all right in those clothes? I mean, they didn't get too wet, did they?"

Jenny inspected her clothing, making a vain attempt to

smooth out the wrinkles. "No, that raincoat of yours did a good job of keeping me dry."

Then she came to the burnt hem of her dress. She stopped, staring at the charred binding as she fought to hold the tears rising in her eyes. Suddenly, she flung the hem from her hands as if she had found herself handling a serpent instead of some scorched fabric. Slowly she lifted her eyes to Cody.

"You might keep an eye on these beans, Cody boy. I'm gonna see what's holdin' up the mail."

Except for the sounds of the fire crackling in the belly of the iron stove and the distant rumbling of thunder, a heavy silence permeated the room following Boz's departure.

"Are you all right? Can I get you anything while we're waitin' on them beans?" Cody asked.

Jenny inhaled sharply, then emitted a mournful sigh as she folded her hands on the tabletop. "I can't believe this isn't some awful nightmare."

"I'm sorry, Jenny. I wish I could say or do something to change what's happened. And unfortunately, it ain't close to bein' over."

"You really think Murphy's coming?"

"Him and every one of those varmints that hit that train this mornin'. He knows once we get to a place where there's any kinda law he's done for, along with his whole gang. They can't afford to let us go."

"He'll have to kill me to stop me," she said defiantly. "I want to see him hang for what he's done."

Cody sat quietly. He wanted to reassure her that the outlaw would hang, but he didn't have that confidence. Law in these parts was scarce. As for the army, he had heard the western outposts were reducing their numbers, sending many of the regular troops back east to fight against the Secessionists while leaving much of the local military affairs in the hands of state and territorial militia.

Besides, he doubted they had the time to wait for any representative of the law to help them against Murphy.

"Well, Jenny, I want to see that renegade answer for what he's done, but don't let bitterness and revenge poison you. My pa warned me with his dying breath not to give bitterness ground to take root in. He said it became a disease that ate a man up from the inside out, so's he wouldn't even recognize a chance for new happiness to ease the old pain." He reached across the table, taking her hands. "I reckon it's a lot the same for a woman too."

Jenny examined his rough, calloused hands carefully. She saw the scars of hard work etched upon their deeply tanned backs. She clasped his hands between hers, then raised her eyes to him.

"Why did he say that to you?"

"My ma and pa were murdered, too."

# CHAPTER 14

CODY withdrew his hands as he stood. His damp clothes clung to his body and he wanted to crawl out of them and dry out. Instead, he moved closer to the stove.

He hadn't told anyone about his folks and he hadn't meant to tell Jenny. It had just occurred to him it might help her to know someone else had experienced that same loss and the words had slipped out before he had a chance to even think about them.

"Can you tell me what happened?"

The pot of beans on the stove began simmering and Cody picked up a wooden spoon and gave them a stir.

"I was seventeen at the time and had just come back from freightin' a load of goods out to Salt Lake. I had some time on my hands and figgered to see my folks over in Missouri. I was drivin' out of Leavenworth at the time.

"It seems there was always some kind of trouble brewin' between the free-staters and slavers, even back then. Somehow my folks got mistaken for bein' property holders and a passel of redlegs crossed the line to teach 'em a lesson."

"Did your folks own—slaves?"

Cody shook his head sadly as he laid the spoon down and turned to face Jenny. "Nary a one. Thing of it is, my pa was always tellin' us boys what an abomination slavery is. But sometimes when a man's blood gets to boilin' he don't wanna listen to talk. And that's the way it is with them border raiders on both sides of the line.

"Anyway, I'd been home nearly a week when Ma sent me to deliver some pullets to a widow lady on the neigh-

109

borin' farm. She told me I should ask the woman if she needed any help with chores and such."

He chuckled wearily as he returned to the table and sat down. He crossed his arms on the tabletop, hunching his shoulders as he leaned forward.

"I ended up spendin' my whole day mendin' chicken wire and hangin' gates . . . The sun was long gone by the time I started back home."

He bowed his head and closed his eyes, fighting the emotion that swelled within his breast, surprised at the effect his reminiscing had on him. Cody exhaled sharply and cleared his throat.

"I smelled smoke long before I saw the flames. By the time I realized where it was comin' from, I was on a dead run for home. I come into the yard and it was like the fires of hell had broken loose. The house was burnin', the barn had already collapsed, and dead animals were layin' everywhere. I couldn't even get close to the front door, so I circled around the house to see if I could find a way in. That's when I found my pa. He'd been beaten real bad and gut shot. When I asked him where Ma was he just nodded toward the barn. He told me to get word to my brothers and get on back to Leavenworth. That's when he warned me about the root of bitterness."

He raised his head, his blue eyes clear and hard. "I swear, I've tried to follow his advice ever since. But maybe it's tougher for you because you've got a name and a face to hate. I never knew who murdered my folks. It was just a part of the hard times we lived in."

"You said you had brothers to tell?"

He had brothers all right. Three of them. And all three, older than Cody, had ignored their father's dying instruction, joining a band of bushwhackers along the Kansas-Missouri border. He had heard nothing from them in three years.

"Yeah, they're off fightin' in the war."

"What about you? Are you going to join the army?"

Cody hadn't given that much thought. He figured to ride the Pony as long the company let him. He had heard some rumors that the Express was in some kind of money trouble, and suspected that the problems were due in part to the relentless advance of the transcontinental telegraph. He knew its completion would signal the demise of the Pony, its tapping key hammering nails into the coffin lid of the Pony Express.

"Right now I'll just keep carryin' the mail. And you? What will you do now?"

"Why, I don't actually know. My grandmother still lives back in Ohio, but there really isn't anything for me to go back to there. I would just be a burden to her."

"Didn't you tell me your pa had a brother out west somewhere? Denver, wasn't it?"

She nodded. "He runs a hotel there and offered my father a half interest in it. He said that once we got settled, father could start another hardware business if he wanted."

"Would you be welcome there?"

"In Denver? I'm sure Uncle Bill and Aunt Evie would let me stay with them. I could certainly earn my keep, working in their hotel. Although I'm not quite sure how I would manage to get there."

"If that's where you want to go, I'll see you get there."

Crig stepped through the door, toting a powder keg, followed by Boz, who had a large pack slung over his shoulder.

"Well, we can hold off an army now," Crig said, puffing as he eased the keg to the floor near the bunks.

Boz dropped the bag of lead balls and it landed with a thud on the dirt floor beside the keg.

"Josh has got the mail on its way again," Boz said as he brushed his hands together. "I sent Emory to scout around some, south of us."

A hissing steam arose from the stove behind Cody.

"Cody! Them beans is boilin' over!"

Lunging from his chair, Cody grabbed a bleached-out remnant of a feed sack and removed the steaming pot from the stove.

"Sorry, Boz. I guess I wasn't payin' much attention to cookin'."

Boz threw a glance at Jenny, then looked again at Cody.

"No harm done. Besides, I reckon I wouldn't give a hoot about some boilin' beans if I was in the company of such a pretty lady."

Jenny blushed.

"Set them beans down, Cody boy," Boz said as he circled the table. "I'll whip up some johnnycake to go along with 'em."

Boz busied himself preparing the yellow corn meal, while Crig sat down on one of the bunks and began loading a pair of Spencer carbines.

Cody settled back into his chair. He drew the two Colts from his sash, along with their two spare cylinders and his knife, and laid them on the table. Then he loosened the bright red cloth around his waist and hung it on the back of his chair to dry out. The Pony rider inspected the revolvers, removing the cylinders from each one, and checking the loads. He did the same with the spares, as he didn't want to take a chance on carrying wet powder in his guns if, indeed, trouble was coming.

Jenny's eyes roved from Crig and Cody working with their firearms, to Boz at the stove. She scooted back from the table and walked to Boz's side.

"I don't know a lot about guns, but I do know something about cooking. Maybe I should see to this while you help . . ." Her voice trailed off as she nodded her head toward the other two men.

Boz grinned.

"Cody boy," he said as he winked at Jenny. "This here is a pretty sharp gal. I'd keep my eye on her if I was you."

"I'd already given that some thought, Boz."

The stationmaster guffawed.

"You know, Miss Jenny, you was rescued by one of Russell, Majors and Waddell's best? Why, Cody is said to be one of the finest horsemen ridin' the prairie. Some even say he's part Injun."

Jenny smiled, noticing Cody didn't look up as he fiddled with his guns.

"I had no idea," she said softly.

By the time Cody joined the Pony Express he had acquired a widespread reputation among the teamsters as a courageous and experienced plainsman. His friendship with Pop McCready, a former Rocky Mountain trapper, had enhanced his standing with his fellow bullwhackers. Pop had instructed him in the art of survival on the prairie, how to read tracks and animal droppings like the printed words on a page, a skill he had acquired during his long trading association with the Crow on the Yellowstone. McCready had just begun teaching him sign language when Cody left to join the Pony.

Cody had also become adept at handling the Remington he had always carried in his sash. He could draw the gun with the deadly speed and accuracy of a striking rattlesnake, though this was a fact few people knew, except for Pop and John Butler. He had never killed anyone and preferred to settle disputes, when words just couldn't smooth things over, with his fists in a good, old-fashioned dogfight.

In his early days as a teamster, chiefly due to his small wiry frame, he found himself the object of derision by many of his brawny peers and forced to defend his honor, but their size hadn't deterred him from standing up to them. Of course, he lost more altercations than he won, but seldom did a fight end without him gaining the respect of his opponent and, in many cases, friendship.

Cody tried not to take his fame among the teamsters too seriously, figuring he had done nothing more than anyone else would do. His mother had always advised him to do his absolute best, no matter what the task, and he had adhered to her instruction for as long as he could remember.

Once the johnnycake finished frying, Jenny sliced generous portions of the yellow bread for Cody and herself, arranging them on battered tin plates, then she ladled beans from the steaming pot. She set one of the plates at Cody's elbow as he snapped the ramrod into place after loading the last cylinder.

"Thanks, Jenny," he said as he scooted the plate over the rough tabletop to sit in front of him.

"You're welcome," she said, handing him a fork. She turned to Crig and Boz. "Can I fill a plate for you? There's plenty here."

The two exchanged glances, then nodded.

"We'd appreciate it, Miss Jenny," Boz said.

She filled two more plates and gave one to each of them before sitting down at the table, opposite Cody. "Do you know when I'll be able to go on to Denver?"

Cody looked up as he pushed beans onto his fork with the cornbread. "The stage is due by here in a coupla days. You oughta be able to take it to Julesburg, then catch the stage to Denver from there."

"But they'll be here before then, won't they?"

Cody held his fork in midair, juice dripping onto the plate. He laid the utensil down. He knew they had a little while before Murphy and his men showed up, but he anticipated their arrival as surely as he expected the sun to set and rise again.

"I'm not gonna lie to you. We're not out of the woods yet. I'm hopin' while Emory's scoutin' out there he runs into John and Everett, but we can't count on that." He cast a quick look past Jenny's shoulder at Boz and Crig. Both men sat on the lower bunks, heads down as they shoveled the food into their mouths. Neither man lifted his head, or raised his voice to contradict him. He took their silence as agreement.

Jenny smiled bravely. "I guess we'll be ready for them."

"You can count on that. Eh, Boz?"

The stationmaster's head snapped up, his black eyes shining. "Yes, sir, we'll send them boys packin' back where they come from, all right."

Emory Tatum leaned over the saddle horn, staring between his horse's ears. He had ridden southeast from the station, then started to swing west, moving slowly, his eyes scanning the rolling prairie. The downpour had finally subsided to a light rainfall about half an hour out of the station, considerably improving visibility, and before another thirty minutes had passed, he had topped a rise, spotting a large band of riders coming in his direction. He didn't hesitate a moment, but slowly wheeled his mount down the low hill, hoping he hadn't been seen. Once off the skyline he spurred his horse eastward. If the riders had sighted him, he didn't want to lead them straight back to Freemont Springs.

His steed galloped over the muddy plain for a couple of miles, then made a beeline north for the river, where he turned back west, heading for the Pony station. Emory quirted his horse and the animal stretched out low over the prairie, its hoofs chewing up the muddy turf. Less than an hour had passed when Tatum spied the station house ahead.

Upon reaching the station, Emory sprang from his saddle and sprinted for the door. Crig Rogers flung it open.

"Did you find 'em?" Crig asked as he stepped aside to let Emory in.

The rider burst through the doorway, coming face to face with Boz and Cody, who stood in the middle of the cabin. Jenny stood near the stove, kneading an old feed-sack dishtowel in her hands.

"They're almost due south of here," Tatum panted. "They're comin' slow. May be another hour 'fore they get here."

"Did they see you?" Cody inquired.

Emory shook his head vigorously. "I don't think so. I was tryin' to be real sneaky."

"Well, sit down, boy," Boz ordered. "Catch yer breath. Crig, look to his horse."

Crig started out the door.

"And keep yer eyes open out there!" the stationmaster commanded.

Emory dropped into a chair at the table and pushed his hat back on his head. His gaze drifted from Boz to Cody and back again.

"There's a bunch of 'em comin'," he said softly.

"How many, do you reckon?" Cody asked.

"Dunno. Might be twenty or so. I didn't take a lot of time to count."

Jenny filled a plate with food and set it on the table in front of Emory.

"Much obliged, Miz Jenny."

"You're welcome."

Cody saw the color had left Jenny's face, though that look of determination he had seen before in her eyes had returned. A smile twisted the corners of his mouth. One thing about this girl, she had a lot of sand.

# CHAPTER 15

CHARILLO backed off the hilltop, then scampered down
the hill to where Big Joe Murphy stood next to his horse.

"Well?" Murphy asked.

"Looks like a relay station. Probably Pony Express,"
Charillo said.

"Think they're in there?"

Charillo shrugged. "If they kept goin' northwest they're
there. Only way we'll know for sure is to ride in there."

Murphy didn't like that idea. This situation called for
delicate maneuvering, not a headlong charge. If the girl
and whoever she rode with had taken refuge within the
station, they would certainly have informed its residents of
the attack on the wagon train. No, he didn't dare ride in
there with the whole gang.

"I got no desire to ride into an ambush," Murphy said.

"Maybe send one man."

"I like the sound of that better." And Murphy knew who
that one man would be. He spun away from the Comanche,
stepped into the stirrup, and hoisted himself onto the
roan's back. Grasping the bight of the reins, he turned the
stallion toward the column. He rode its length until he
reached Ike bringing up the rear.

"Got a job for ya, Ike," he said evenly.

"I'm a-listenin'."

"Charillo thinks he's led us to that gal. Looks like she's
holed up at a relay station the other side of that hill."

Ike nodded as he gazed at the mound before them. "I'm
still listenin'."

Big Joe squinted his left eye, but didn't let his temper

flare. He was certain Ike knew what he wanted him to do and didn't understand Pappas's attitude. They had ridden together since the Battle of San Jacinto, when, hardly more than boys, they had fought in the war for Texas independence. Ike had been with him when he had found the gold medallion that he carried for luck, and Big Joe had always thought of Ike as part of that good fortune. It was incomprehensible to Murphy that Ike had wearied of his bullying, for he had always given the orders and Ike had invariably carried them out.

"Want ya to ride on over and make sure she's there," he said, struggling to keep his mounting anger in check.

Ike tugged the brim of his hat down as he stared at his saddle horn. "Reckon I could do that," he said without looking up.

"Well, if it wouldn't put ya out too much, I'd appreciate it," Murphy growled. "I'll be waitin' for ya."

Big Joe whirled the roan about and started along the column, telling his men to hold up while Ike checked the station up ahead.

Ike walked his horse past the others without giving anyone so much as a glance. He rode by as if he shared the prairie with no one else.

Murphy fumed as Ike rode by without any sign of acknowledgment. He jumped from his saddle and, turning to his men, signalled them to do likewise. Then he returned his attention to Ike's shrinking back.

"Ever'body might as well slide off yer saddles," he said.

Charillo trotted his horse over to Murphy. "Ike rides slow today."

"You'd think he's racin' snails and wanted them to win."

The Indian nodded thoughtfully. "Ike don't like the job you give him, huh?"

"No, I reckon he don't. You ride on up that hill yonder and keep an eye on them cabins. When Ike gets inside I want ya to slip down there and do a little nosin' around. Maybe you'll find somethin' he don't."

Charillo jerked his mount's reins and galloped away.

Cody drummed his fingers on the rough tabletop, chafing under the oppressive silence that had descended upon the station. He forced himself to sit in his chair, remembering Pop McCready's warnings about the dangers of impatience. An anxious man risked acting recklessly, endangering himself and those who counted on his help in a time of trouble. He knew he must subdue the restlessness within him and keep his mind alert.

The rain had finally ended and the late-afternoon sun drifted lazily above the horizon, unable to reclaim its preeminence over the day. The storm that had cooled the afternoon left its legacy to the early evening, and a gentle, refreshing breath floated across the prairie. The blue shadows of corral posts pointed like slender fingers at the approaching nightfall and from that encroaching darkness came the mournful call of a wolf. The horses in the corral lifted their heads at the cry and nickered uncomfortably, ears pricked toward the howling.

Crig heard the horses and went out to investigate. He checked the ropes of the corral, making sure they held fast. He stood in the quiet dusk, listening for the wolf, but another sound intruded. His eyes rapidly swept the prairie and immediately spotted an advancing rider. He let his gaze glide over the horseman as if he hadn't seen him and started for the headquarters. Crig sauntered across the yard as careless as a cat. When he reached the cabin he entered without so much as a glance behind him.

"Heads up!" he whispered, closing the door behind him.

Everyone came to their feet like a church choir on Sunday morning.

"There's a rider comin' in real slow."

"Did you recognize him?" Boz asked.

Rogers shook his head.

"I didn't get a good look at him."

Cody wiped the back of his hand across his mouth, then looked at Jenny.

"Could be somebody Murphy sent ahead. I think you oughta hide under one of the bunks."

"Too close to the floor," Boz said. "Just jump in one of 'em and yank the kivers up over yer head."

Jenny hurriedly crossed the room and crawled into one of the beds, covering herself with a blanket.

"All right," Cody said as he sat down again at the table. "Reckon we'll just let this fella ankle in and offer him a bean. So everybody just rest easy."

Crig and Emory sat at the table with Cody, and Crig began shuffling a dogeared deck of cards. He had just started dealing when a light knock sounded at the door.

"Hello, in the house!" Ike Pappas hollered.

Boz ambled to the door and drew it open. "Evenin', mister. What can I do for you?"

"Got caught in that cussed storm this afternoon and lost my bearin's. What's this place?"

"This here is the Freemont Springs station of the Pony Express, where supper's over, but there's still coffee on the stove. It'll shore take the chill outa you."

"Mighty kind of ya. I think I'll take ya up on that offer."

Cody and the others at the table greeted Ike as he came through the door.

"Pull up a chair," Crig offered as he stood. "I'll fetch you that coffee."

"Thanks," Ike said. His eyes darted furtively around the room before taking a chair at the table. "So this is a relay station?"

"Finest on the line," Boz said, laughing.

His quick survey hadn't escaped Cody's attention, and the Pony rider knew this man belonged to the same bunch that had wiped out the Rutheford train. Cody kept a smile pasted on his lips, all the while yearning to draw a pistol and poke it in the killer's face and demand to know Murphy's whereabouts. But he kept both his hands on the tabletop, firmly grasping his cards.

Cody stole a swift glance at the stranger's face now and again, wanting to make sure he remembered him when they met in the future. He knew a savage butcher sat across the table from him. He had seen his work.

Boz dragged a powder keg up to the table and eased his bulky frame onto it with a loud groan as Crig set a cup of coffee in front of Ike.

"Name's Bosworth. Folks call me Boz. And this here is Emory Tatum, Crig Rogers, and Cody Bailey."

Ike nodded at each of them. "They call me Pap," he said.

"I heard you tell Boz you got turned around in the storm today?" Emory asked as he threw two of his cards on the table. "I'll take two."

"Yup," Ike grunted. "Darnedest thing. I ain't never got lost in a storm before. And I been caught in some howlers."

"Happened to me once," Cody said. "Got so plumb confused I finally tossed an end of my rope into the Platte to see which way she was a-runnin'. I was all right after that."

"I couldn't even find the river," Ike said with a laugh.

The other men chuckled lightly.

"Where're you headed, Pap?" Crig asked.

"Back home." He tipped the cup to his lips, sipping noisily.

"Where might that be?" Boz inquired innocently.

Ike slowly lowered the tin mug, staring into the black liquid. "You boys ain't got nothin' against Southerners, have ya?"

Boz guffawed loudly.

"You joshin'? Why, man, I'm from Virginia! And I think Cody's from Missouri."

Ike emitted a sigh of relief. "Way things are these days a fella never knows where he might not find a welcome."

"So, yer from the South, are ya?" Boz pressed.

"Yup. Texas."

Cody fought the urge to lunge over the table and throttle Murphy's partner.

Ike finished his coffee and set his cup on the table. He placed his hands palms down on either side of the cup and pushed himself back from the table. "Well, gents, I appreciate yer hospitality, but I best be gettin' along."

"Why, it's purt near dark," Boz said, raising his eyebrows. "No reason to rush off. Yer welcome to spread yer bedroll out on the floor and spend the night. None of us snores too loud that I'm aware of."

The outlaw stood. "Much obliged, but I need to move on."

"Suit yerself."

"Where might you be headin'? I mean, you ain't gonna make Texas tonight," Cody said.

"Just like to keep movin'."

Boz escorted him to the door.

"Watch yer step as you move south," he advised. "You'll be headin' into free-stater country. Ain't likely they'll cotton to someone from yer neck of the woods."

"Thanks. I'll remember that."

The stationmaster accompanied the outlaw outside and saw him onto his horse. His eyes followed the stranger as he rode out of the yard until he disappeared in the growing darkness. Before heading inside, Boz surveyed the station, letting his gaze drift over the corral, the crude stable, and back to the cabins. He turned back to the headquarters.

"Better keep Miz Jenny under wraps a bit longer," he said as he latched the door.

"Somethin' wrong?" Cody asked.

A scowl knitted Boz's shaggy eyebrows. "I dunno. I shore had a feelin' somebody else was out there just now."

"Did you see anybody?" Crig inquired.

"No. No, I didn't. But I think we better keep our eyes open tonight."

"Better post a guard, then," Cody recommended.

Boz nodded. "That's what I was thinkin'. Crig, you'll take the first watch 'til midnight, then wake Emory. I'll take over at two, then Cody can have it from four 'til daybreak. Meantime, ever'body keep their voices low and don't discuss—" He pointed to the bunk where Jenny lay hidden.

Like many of the others that tended the stations along the line, Boz had ridden the plains for several years, working not only as a teamster, but also as an Indian fighter with the Rangers in the Llano country of west Texas. He had learned many hard lessons, as any man in an untamed land must, and he knew the business of staying alive. And because of that, Cody trusted his judgment and didn't hesitate to follow his instructions.

Charillo slithered on his belly among the shadows by the corral. He moved noiselessly over the muddy ground, careful not to disturb the horses. As soon as Ike had entered the house he had circled the station, coming at it from the opposite direction of Ike's approach. He had picketed his horse in a wash about a hundred yards north and walked the rest of the way in. The Comanche had hardly situated himself inside the lean-to when Ike emerged from the cabin with Boz and rode off.

The stationmaster's wariness didn't escape Charillo's attention, and as Boz's gaze passed over the lean-to, the Indian sat as still as a cactus. Then Boz had gone inside and he had relaxed. He sat in a frog squat and studied the cabins. He needed to get a look inside, but that had to wait until full darkness had come, which lessened the risk of someone spotting him as he crossed the yard.

He commenced rocking on his haunches, letting his eyes adjust to the deep shadows within the lean-to. Once he became used to the dim light, he began inspecting his immediate surroundings, a habit he had acquired as a young boy on the southern plains. He had learned the ways of his people in utilizing the land as another weapon in their arsenal and hadn't forgotten the value of that teaching while sojourning among the whites. And keeping those skills honed paid off now, for he spied a familiar horseshoe print in the sandy soil floor of the shed. The same as the one he had found at the site of the emigrant massacre. He carefully traced the outline of the mark with his right index finger. He gazed at the headquarters, lightly tapping the print he had discovered. Then his eyes shifted to the direction Ike had taken out of the yard, his finger still tapping the track. Suddenly he started to leave the lean-to, but just as he moved the sound of approaching horses seized his attention.

Charrillo flopped on his belly and hugged the earth, listening intently to the hoofbeats. He shrank into the darker recesses of the shed, reaching for the bowie sheathed in the top of his moccasin, awaiting the arrival of the horsemen.

A scant moment later two horses raced into the station yard and the Comanche immediately spied the two men the gang had encountered among the ruins of the wagon train.

# CHAPTER 16

CRIG Rogers raced to the window nearest the bunks when he heard the horses gallop into the yard. He peered into the darkness, then turned to the inquiring faces behind him.

"It's John and Everett."

Cody heaved a sigh of relief.

"Good," he said. "We'll probably need the reinforcements."

John and Everett reined their horses to an abrupt halt near the entrance to the station house. Butler threw his right leg over the saddle horn and dropped to the ground. With a few quick strides he reached the cabin's door just as Boz swung it open, bathing John's face in the pale yellow glow of the lamplight.

"C'mon in, Butler," Boz said with a chuckle. "Got a missing friend of yers in here."

"Is Cody here?" John asked as he entered the dusty dwelling.

In answer to his question he saw Bailey standing beside the table, his back to the stove. John yanked his hat from his head and tossed it onto the table as he crossed the room to Cody.

"Man, am I glad to see you. We've been huntin' you all day."

"I'd say it looks like you found me."

"No thanks to you," John said, clapping Cody's shoulders. "We done wore out four horses and half the prairie between here and Parker's Junction trying to track you down."

"Guess you seen what happened at Cold Springs then?"

John's expression became somber. "Yeah, but bad as that was, it was hardly spit on a hot rock compared to the wagon train we came across."

"You saw it too?"

"Followed its smoke, thinkin' we might find you there."

"I was through there, all right."

"We found Champ's hoofprint. Well, anyway, Everett ran across it after we met up with some outfit claimin' to be outa Julesburg."

Cody swung his leg over a chair and sat down at the table, propping his elbows on its top. He laced his fingers together and bowed his forehead against them. "Man leadin' this bunch wouldn't have been a big burly fella with a salt-and-pepper beard?"

John sat down across the table. "As a matter of fact. Ya know him?"

Cody raised his head, peering into John's eyes. "He was that train's pilot."

John's mouth gaped.

Cody related his conversation with Pop McCready about Murphy and his subsequent meeting with Captain Phillip Conway corroborating Pop's suspicions that Murphy was behind the rumored Indian trouble. Then he briefly described the scene he had witnessed upon reaching the wagons and Jenny's rescue.

"Where's the girl now?"

"Hidin' yonder," Cody said, inclining his head toward the bunks. "We figure she's still in a heap of trouble."

"Reckon you're right, 'cause them boys were headed this way. Me and Everett didn't quite buy into their story 'bout bein' from Julesburg, and when we found Champ's track we had a feelin' you might be in trouble."

"Not yet, but one of 'em showed up here, nosin' around. I think we threw him off the scent, but"—Cody shook his head—"I'm not real sure. Did you see 'em on your way in?"

John glanced around the room at Boz, Crig, and Emory, then set his eyes on Cody.

"No, and we made a point of avoidin' 'em. We rode hard to get here, but then, we were sure this was where you were headed." He took a deep breath. "Must be nearly twenty of them. Odds ain't exactly tilted in our favor."

"Josh Carpenter took the mail on to Elkhorn. He'll be sendin' along some help."

Bailey gazed at John. He didn't know how much help to expect from Elkhorn. They employed a smaller staff than Boz used at Freemont Springs, and though Cody didn't say it, he doubted anyone could reach them in time to provide any assistance if Murphy decided to move against them tonight. However, Cody thought that their performance before Murphy's cohort had accomplished its purpose and had bought them more time. At least he hoped so.

"How 'bout some coffee, John?" Boz asked, crossing the dirt floor. "Should still have some in the pot."

"Yeah, thanks, Boz," he said, then turned in his chair, studying the door. "Sure is takin' Everett a long time with them horses."

"I'll see what's keepin' him," Crig volunteered and headed out the door, cradling a Spencer rifle in the hollow of his left arm. The door had hardly closed behind him when a shot rang out, quickly followed by two more.

John leapt to his feet, hat in hand, and scrambled for the exit. Cody slapped on his own headgear and followed. They halted on either side of the door frame, guns at the ready. Just as John reached for the handle, the door burst open and Crig lunged over the threshold, clutching his belly as he collapsed on the floor.

Boz cast the rifle he had grabbed onto one of the empty bunks and rushed to Crig's side.

"Help me get him to the bed," he said to Emory.

Jenny poked her head from beneath the tattered quilt. "What is it? What's happening?"

"Get back under there!" Cody ordered.

She scowled at him, but pulled the cover over her head again.

Crouching low, John crossed the sill into the yard, with Cody close behind him. They heard the sound of the horses milling restlessly in the corral and nothing else.

Cody tapped John's arm and leaned close to his ear.

"Let's circle around behind the stable," he whispered. "You go left. I'll go right."

John nodded as he began moving away.

"Spurs!" Cody hissed as he removed his and laid them next to the station house. John followed suit.

The muddy ground of the station yard sucked at Cody's boots, impairing his ability to move quietly. He edged away from the station until he reached the grass that surrounded it, then rapidly circled the yard, coming up behind the corral. He crept toward the lean-to, then halted, his eyes sweeping the dark prairie to his right for a sign of John, but he didn't see him. He moved forward, slipping between the ropes that encompassed the corral, and threaded his way among the horses.

The animals had settled down since the shooting and the crickets had begun their evening serenade. The tail of the ink-black storm clouds wavered on the eastern horizon, while glittering stars filled the sky overhead. Out on the prairie an owl hooted as it commenced its nightly hunt.

Cody reached the shed and peered inside to see Everett Samuels sprawled in the dust, his throat slit wide, the gray and the buckskin standing beside him, still saddled. Cody stood motionless, studying every inch of the lean-to for any conceivable hiding place. Several feed sacks were stacked in the far corner behind Everett's body, and Cody saw them as providing the most likely site for concealment.

He stepped cautiously beneath the sod roof, his eyes fixed on the opposite corner. He doubted Everett's killer remained in the shed, but he drew near the mound of bags as if approaching a nest of rattlesnakes. Upon reaching the sacks he discovered just what he had expected. Nothing. Whoever had murdered Everett had already made his escape.

Kneeling beside his lifeless comrade, Cody inspected the loose dirt floor. The struggle appeared to have been brief. The killer must have surprised Everett, as the dead stockman's pistol still rested in its holster and neither of the horses had been secured to the hitch rings that lined the back wall of the ramshackle building.

Suddenly Cody heard several shots outside the shed. He leapt to his feet and raced into the yard. He heard more shots coming from the north. He scurried back into the lean-to, thrusting his Colt into his sash, grabbed the reins of both horses, and led them into the yard. Still clutching the gray's bridle straps, he vaulted into the buckskin's saddle and drove his heels into the horse's flanks as he pointed him northward. He hunched low over the saddle horn, cocking his head as he listened for more gunfire.

John had nearly reached the lean-to when he spotted Charillo dashing through the grass behind the shelter. He took after him at a dead run, but the Indian saw him and began shooting. John returned the fire, squeezing off a couple of rounds before diving into the grass. He rolled to his left, came up firing his pistol where he had last seen Murphy's scout, then flopped onto the ground again.

As he slowly raised his head, John's eyes bore into the darkness, but he saw no sign of Charillo. The Indian had disappeared. He heard hoofs pounding the level behind him, but didn't turn his head. He saw the stab of fire from the revolver's muzzle and a brief glimpse of the Indian's silhouette. He fired at the renegade.

Cody pulled hard on the reins and lunged from the

saddle, dodging Charillo's bullet as it hummed past his ear. He lay motionless in the damp grass, the two horses less than ten feet from him, their heads up and ears pricked forward. Then he heard the galloping of a horse in the distance and leapt to his feet. He knew Everett's killer rode that horse.

"Johnny!"

"Over here!"

Leading the horses, Cody followed the sound of Butler's voice and found the stockman standing a few yards ahead of him.

"You all right?" Cody asked.

"Sure. And you?"

"Not a scratch."

"Do we go after him? He looked like the Indian that found Champ's print back at the train."

"Well, then, he's headed for Murphy, no doubt."

"He ain't got that much of a lead. And I'm pretty sure I hit him. That oughta slow him up a mite. Besides, I see you brought two horses."

Cody wondered what Murphy would do if his man didn't come back. He might assume the Pony Express men had the girl and attack the station. However, if his spy reached him, Cody had no doubts concerning the pilot's actions. He had to stop the Indian from contacting the outlaw.

"Let's try and follow him. Did you see which direction he headed?"

"East, along that cut."

"East?"

Cody didn't like the sound of that, figuring the bandits would have been south of the depot. Perhaps the outlaws had surrounded the station. Did he dare leave Jenny with only Boz and Emory to protect her?

"If we're gonna try and catch up with that rascal we better get ridin' now."

"Let's go."

The two mounted their horses and rode into the shallow, narrow ravine.

"Everett was dead?" John asked from behind Cody.

"Yep. The Indian slit his throat."

"The rotten savage."

"Looked like he died quick."

"That's the way I'd want it."

"Me too, I reckon."

They rode along the wash in silence for half an hour, with no sign of Charillo. Cody searched the rain-softened earth for telltale tracks, dismounting twice to search the bench, but the moonless night deprived him of much-needed light. He had decided to give up and return to the station when he spotted a break in the low wall of the gulch. He swung to the ground, examining the churned soil.

"That him?"

Cody nodded, sifting the damp soil between his fingers.

"I knew it!" he bellowed as he hurled the dirt from his hand.

"What?"

"He's headed south. He suckered us away from the station, then headed for Murphy."

Cody mounted the buckskin and dug his heels into its ribs, prodding the animal up the embankment and onto the flat. Butler charged out of the ravine behind him. The two men goaded their horses to a gallop, heading for the Pony station. The hooves of the animals pounded the earth as the riders crouched low in the saddles.

The Indian had outsmarted him. He should never have left Jenny, no matter who had stayed with her. He had assumed the burden of responsibility for her safety and now he feared he had let her down, leaving her to face the murderous pilot. And what about Boz? And Emory and Crig? He had made them a party to all of this, too.

Murphy's spy would do his best to ensure their deaths just as he had Everett's.

"Cody!"

John's yell jolted him from his self-reproach and he reined to a halt. John pulled up beside him.

"What is it?"

John pointed ahead.

"Oh, no," Cody said in anguish as he saw the faint glow in the western sky. They were too late! Murphy had struck the Pony station.

As they sat transfixed, staring at the red-orange light before them, a low rumble reached their ears. Cody turned to John.

"Reckon that would be the extra powder Crig brought in to fight off the bandits."

He whipped the buckskin's shoulders with the bight of the reins as he dug in his heels.

"C'mon! Let's go!"

By the time they reached the station all that remained of the twin huts was twisted, burning wreckage. None of the horses remained and the lean-to had collapsed.

Cody and John stood, reins in hand, staring into the searing inferno. The soaring flames bred shadows that leapt and writhed like the ghosts of primeval dancers in the station yard. Cody felt an oppressive weight settle on his chest as though unseen bands of iron had encircled his ribs. He took a deep breath, swelling his breast in a vain attempt to rend the invisible bonds.

"Guess we better take a look around," he said, sighing. "See if we can find which way they headed."

They retrieved their spurs and slipped them on, then began their search of the station yard.The fire illuminated an abundance of hoofprints, but it didn't take Cody and John long to sort them out. The main body of outlaws had gone back south, while a smaller contingent had taken out west. Among the prints that pointed south, Cody recognized one of the notched shoes.

"What do you make of all this?" John asked.

"Well, it would appear that at least one of our people got away and Murphy sicked some of his dogs on 'em."

"The girl?"

Cody shook his head. "I don't think so. My guts tell me Murphy's got her."

"So, now what?"

"Reckon you better get after this bunch," he said, pointing at the trail that headed west. "Whoever they're chasin' is gonna need some help if they can't outrun 'em."

"I take it that means you're goin' after the main bunch."

"Yep. That's what it means all right."

John extended his hand and Cody grasped it firmly.

"You keep your eyes open, Johnny."

"I'll be comin' as soon as I send these boys to see St. Peter."

"I'll be watchin' for you."

Cody turned away and stepped into the saddle. He tipped his hat at John, then spurred the buckskin into the night.

# CHAPTER 17

JOHN swung onto the gray's back, yanking the reins to turn the animal westward. The horse galloped away from the blazing station, following the westward trail that led from the yard. John had ridden nearly five miles when he heard the first shots. He slowed his horse to a trot as he neared the gunfire and a moment later saw the first flashes of fire leaping from the gun muzzles still concealed in the darkness.

Reining the gray to a halt, John slipped from the saddle and drew his pistol. He checked the loads, then began walking stealthily toward the gunfight.

It was a clear, moonless night, and the stars sparkled like slivers of glass against the black velvet sky as John inched his way through the choking gray ghost of spent powder that swirled in the air. No breeze stirred to cleanse the atmosphere of the heavy, pungent odor of sulfur that tainted each breath, burning his throat as he drew it in.

A barrage of gunfire erupted directly ahead of him, rumbling like thunder. A brief quiet ensued, broken when a couple of shots spat fire and lead to his right. He gazed through the whirling gun smoke toward the spot where the reports had come from. John began moving to his left, circling behind the band of gunmen in front of him.

Emory Tatum and Crig Rogers had taken refuge atop a grassy knoll overlooking the trail to Elkhorn. Unable to outrun the outlaws pursuing them, they had halted their flight to make a final stand beside the road.

Crig's belly wound had incapacitated him. Even now he

lay unconscious beside Emory, who had the stock of his Spencer carbine nestled against his shoulder and his Colt and Crig's Remington resting on the ground before him. Sweat dripped from the end of Emory's nose as he stared hard into the gunsmoke below him. He threw a swift glance at his companion.

"I think we're in a mess of trouble here," he said to his comatose friend.

Crig had begged Emory to leave him behind when their pursuers had closed in on them, but Emory had refused, expressing his resolve to stick with Crig to the end. He turned his attention once again to the smoky fog below him.

Out in the darkness John Butler slipped up on the nest of outlaws. He counted five blue shadows crouched in the grass, their faces turned toward the knoll where the insignificant shots had come from just moments before. He sank to his hands and knees and began crawling toward them, clutching his pistol in his hand. As he neared the harbingers of death he overheard a rising argument.

". . . and I say we mount up and rush 'em," one of the men growled.

"Just risk gettin' somebody killed."

"I vote we just grab our horses and git!" a third shadow hollered.

Silence fell over the group. John backed away, glancing one way then the other as he searched for the outlaws' horses. He found them picketed less than ten yards away. He untied the animals and began leading them away from the desperados' position. Once he had put some distance between himself and the brigands, he began howling and yipping like a coyote as he waved his hat and fired his gun into the air. The horses bolted, charging headlong into the empty prairie. John scurried for his own horse, the enraged curses of the horseless miscreants ringing in his ears.

He swung aboard the gray, wheeling it toward the knoll as he spurred its flanks. He hunched low in the saddle, laying his cheek against the horse's neck as he neared the rise. A shot from the mound sent a bullet singing past his right shoulder.

"Hold your fire," he called to Emory. "Don't shoot! It's Butler! I've got help!"

Emory lowered the Spencer as he heard John's declaration. A moment later a horse bounded over the hilltop.

"Man, you should have hollered sooner! I could've blown your head off!" Emory looked around. "Where's the rest of your help?"

"I'm all there is. That was for the benefit of them bushwhackers down yonder. Can you ride?"

"Sure, I can ride," Tatum responded, then pointed at Crig. "But I don't think he can."

"Is he dead?"

"Not yet."

John hopped from the saddle and hustled to Crig's side. He dropped to his knees beside the stockman, then bent his ear to his chest, listening intently. John sat up and pulled the blood-soaked bandage away to expose Crig's wound. He whistled low.

"I can't believe he's still breathin'."

"I ain't leavin' without him," Emory asserted.

John nodded. "I wouldn't have expected otherwise. Have you still got his horse?"

"At the foot of the hill, but Crig ain't in no shape to ride."

"Well, then we'll just have to throw him over his saddle, but we have got to get outa here. I chased them boys' horses off and I haven't any idea how much time that'll buy us."

"Are ya crazy? We might as well put a bullet in his brain

and be done with it. Ridin' like that is sure to land him in a shallow grave."

"We can't just sit here. You know that."

Emory stared at his white-faced comrade. "Maybe we could rig up one of them Injun contraptions. You know, with the long poles and blankets."

"It's pitch dark. Where we gonna find any poles? Look, let's just lay him over his saddle and try and get him to Elkhorn as quick as we can."

"Reckon that's about all we can do," Emory finally agreed.

They hauled Crig down the hillside, gently laying him over the saddle of his horse. John retrieved a coil of rope from the gray's saddle, tied one end around Crig's ankles, ran the line under the horse's belly, then bound his wrists with the other end. Once they had secured Rogers, they mounted their own horses and started for Elkhorn.

"What happened to Boz and the girl?"

Emory hung his head, shaking it slowly as he began his tale. . . .

Boz had sat in the hut after closing the door behind Cody and John, listening attentively to every sound. After they heard gunfire, the stationmaster had forced himself to wait five minutes before going outside to find out what had happened. Finally, when he went out, he discovered Everett's body in the shed but no sign of Cody or John.

He hurried back to the cabin, ordering Emory to saddle horses for everyone, while he scrambled to fill a sack with grub. Upon his return from the lean-to, Emory found Boz and Jenny wrapping Crig in a blanket.

"Help me get him on a horse," Boz ordered.

Emory dutifully followed Boz's instructions and assisted him in carrying Crig outside. Jenny followed them, toting the food sack the beefy expressman had filled.

"Where we headed?" Emory asked as they sat Crig on a horse.

"Best bet is to make for Elkhorn. If Josh was able to send help maybe we'll run into them."

"Leave me behind, Boz," Crig murmured. "I'll just slow you down. Get you all killed."

"Hush, boy."

As Emory swung onto his horse a deep rumble rolled in from the prairie like the distant thunder of an approaching storm.

"Boz?"

"I hear it. Get goin'! Me and the gal will be right behind you!"

Emory spurred his horse and, clutching the reins of Crig's mount, struck out into the night. . . .

Emory stared at John Butler's silhouette as they rode side by side.

"I don't know how far we'd gone before I realized Boz and Jenny weren't catchin' up. And about that time them other fellas did. They opened fire on us and we broke for cover. Next thing I know you come ridin' up that hill. Sure is a good thing you come along when ya did."

"I'll ride with you to Elkhorn, then I'm goin' after Cody."

"Reckon he went after the lady?"

"He did. Odds are against him, that's for sure. But when he's riled, Cody can be meaner than a basket of snakes. And he don't wear that brace of Colts for decoration."

"Mighty handy, is he?"

"That's a fact."

Cody wound his way along the twisting arroyo, leading the buckskin as the sun rose above the horizon. He had sighted the thin, spiraling column of gray smoke a half hour before, after following the tracks of Murphy's cutthroats through the night. They had left a trail that had rolled out like a scroll before him. In fact, Cody had expected a trap, figuring Murphy had left such a clear trail for that specific purpose, but the ambush had never come.

Cody stood beside the buckskin, gently stroking the animal's muzzle as he searched the gully for a place to picket him. He spotted the exposed root of a dead cottonwood protruding from the bank and tied the horse there. He drew one of the Colts from his sash and proceeded along the arroyo, crouching low to avoid detection by those on the bench above.

When he drew close enough to catch fragments of conversations and smell the aroma of brewing coffee, Cody swept his hat off and dropped it at his feet, then peeked over the edge of the bench. Although the sun had risen nearly an hour before, many of the men still lay sleeping in their bedrolls. A small group of the outlaws congregated around the lone campfire, sipping coffee from banged-up tin cups. Cody gathered from the snippets of discussion he overheard that not all of Murphy's men were happy, though his eavesdropping failed to provide him with the reason for their displeasure.

Cody turned his attention from the men at the fire, scanning the rest of the camp for Murphy, figuring Jenny would be close by. Then he saw her on the opposite side of the camp, kneeling beside a blanket-wrapped figure and holding a cup in her hand. Cody remembered that John had thought he'd shot Murphy's Indian back at the Pony station; perhaps it was him in the blanket.

Cody retreated into the gap. Up ahead, the arroyo turned sharply eastward, away from the outlaw encampment. He saw no way to reach Jenny without exposing himself to the bandits and he dared not risk that. He would have to stay on their trail and hope for a better opportunity.

Cody bent over and retrieved his hat, settling it atop his

head. He turned to start back to his horse, but halted, suddenly sensing he wasn't the only one in this wash. He hadn't heard anything, yet he knew someone else was near. Cody began moving toward his horse again, his eyes sweeping the bed of the gap and the banks above him. Straining his ears, he listened for the slightest anomaly in the desert sounds, but he heard nothing.

Creeping stealthily along the arroyo, he neared the bend around which he had left the buckskin. He froze when he saw a dust cloud in the air above the spot where he had tied the gelding. Suddenly he realized his mouth had gone dry. He tried to lick his lips, but they felt like sandpaper against his tongue. His heart pounded in his chest as he studied his next move. Perhaps he ought to sit tight and see if anyone rounded the bend. After all, the buckskin might have kicked up that dust. But what if someone really was there? One of these thieves? They might just make off with the animal, leaving him afoot. No man could afford to be stranded out here without a horse. Cody decided he had no choice.

He moved ahead, choosing each step with care. As he neared the bend, he flattened himself against the side of the gap. A couple more steps and he expected to see the buckskin tethered to the root of the old cottonwood. He was still there.

From where he stood Cody could see the opposite side of the wash where the gelding waited, but not what was around the turn. The horse lifted his head, staring straight at Cody. The Pony rider swallowed hard. Suddenly he lunged against the opposite bank as he thumbed back the hammer of his revolver.

Three of Murphy's men waited in the draw, planning to ambush Cody when he returned for his horse. Their eyes widened with surprise when he leapt unexpectedly into their midst, but they held their guns ready.

Cody's Colt belched lead as he rapidly fired. The first

ball struck the man closest to him beneath the left eye. Cody knew the man was dead as soon as he pulled the trigger, and turned his attention to the second man, firing into his chest. The bandit brought his pistol to bear on Cody, squeezing off his shot at the moment the Pony rider's bullet splintered his breastbone. His shot was wide, but still caught Cody high in his left shoulder.

The impact of the shot staggered Cody and he fell back against the bank. From the corner of his eye he saw the third outlaw raising his gun, but the second man wasn't out of it yet. He had fallen to his knees, still clutching his pistol. And once again he pointed it at Cody.

Not so much thinking as reacting, Cody knew instinctively the unscathed outlaw demanded his attention. The wounded man had taken a severe blow and his reflexes and accuracy would surely suffer. Cody pushed off the embankment, firing his revolver as he pitched himself into the dust.

Three shots sounded as one in the narrow ravine. Before he hit the ground Cody felt the burning lead from the injured outlaw's gun strike his left hip, as the bullet from the other man hummed passed his ear. Cody's own bullet hit the third man in the belly, doubling him over.

Cody scrambled to his feet, covering the bandits with his pistol. One was dead and the other two soon would be. No one moved to interfere with his retreat. He knew he had to get on the buckskin and out of there before any more of the outlaws showed up. He had to get somewhere where he could hole up and find out how badly he had been hit.

# CHAPTER 18

CODY'S eyes fluttered open to behold the star-filled vault above him. His shoulder and hip ached, and when he fingered them he discovered bandages on them. The last thing he remembered was clinging to the saddle horn as he spurred the buckskin across the prairie. He had no memory of falling from his horse, or encountering anyone, though he did recall a wave of nausea and fatigue washing over him as he fled the outlaws' encampment.

The savory aroma of roasting meat filled his nostrils and he struggled to lift himself on his right elbow. A hand reached out from the darkness, grasping his shoulder.

"No move, Co-dee."

He looked up into the black eyes of an Indian squatting next to him.

"Standing Bear?"

The Sioux brave firmly but gently pushed against Cody's shoulder, then, lifting his palms, indicated Cody should lay still. Using sign, he attempted to explain to Cody that he had found him wounded on the prairie and had brought him to the camp of his people, but it was apparent the Pony rider didn't comprehend. Standing Bear stood and walked away.

Cody watched the retreating figure stride across an open yard surrounded by several tipis. Cody thought he recognized the artwork on the dwelling Standing Bear ducked into. As he studied the richly colored decorations, the old man Red Eagle emerged from the structure's opening, followed by the younger man. The ancient warrior stood ramrod straight as he crossed the clearing. He came to a halt beside the wounded Pony rider, then sat cross-legged on the ground beside him.

"You are awake, eh?"

Cody nodded.

"Have not seen Co-dee since Moon of Falling Leaves, when he brought home Standing Bear."

Cody nodded again. "Yes, sir. Last October."

"You shot up now. Not by Sichangus? Not by our people?" He asked, waving his hand to indicate the circle of tipis.

"No. White men. Murderers."

The old man stared over Cody into the starlit night, as though lost in thought. "White man attack you?" he asked, still staring.

"I was chasin' them. I got caught by three of 'em and had to shoot my way out."

"You chase many?"

Cody shrugged. "They killed a bunch of people and kidnapped a girl. Stole her from her family."

"You chase men? Or you chase girl?"

Cody furrowed his brow. "How bad am I hurt?"

"You lucky. Not hurt bad."

"I've got to travel soon. I have to find 'em again."

"Eat now, then rest," the warrior ordered as he stood. "We talk morning."

As the long shadows of dawn emerged from the night, Cody rolled onto his right side, then pushed himself upright. He lifted the buffalo robe that blanketed him and discovered he had no clothes on. He frantically searched the ground about him, but saw no sign of his missing garments. Surveying the camp he saw nothing but a few of the women stirring the coals of last night's fires, heating the stones for boiling water in the paunch kettles outside their tipis.

Cody rolled back his blanket to inspect his injuries. His fingers probed the bandage that saddled his left shoulder.

It wrapped around his chest and back, secured by a knot beneath his right armpit. The thickness of the dressing prevented him from evaluating the damage the bullet had wrought, though one thing he knew for sure, his shoulder ached a lot. He pushed the blanket down farther to reveal his hip. The Indians had applied a greasy salve that smelled of unfamiliar herbs to the wound, which was little more than a crease, the skin barely parted. He noticed there was very little inflammation around the opening and knew that was good.

He gazed across the clearing at the tipi where he had seen Red Eagle come from last night. He was anxious to talk to the warrior and find out how bad his shoulder wound was. He wanted desperately to get back on Murphy's trail.

Cody lay back, gathering the buffalo robe beneath his chin, thinking about his earlier conversation with Red Eagle. Had he taken after Murphy because of the crime he had committed, or because the outlaw had Jenny? He hadn't given that much thought until now, and as he pondered the questions he arrived at the only possible conclusion: he had done it for Jenny. If he had sighted the black column of smoke during the course of his ride, even after encountering the carnage at Cold Springs, he wouldn't have veered from his path. The mail came first with him, as it did with almost every rider. Certainly he would have reported his observation at the next station, but he wouldn't have passed the mail to another to complete his route. For Jenny he had delayed delivery of the mail, in effect breaking his oath to the company. Even though he felt he had no choice, it didn't change that fact. If he was still alive when all of this was done, he planned to return to Parker's Junction and resign.

He saw Red Eagle crossing the yard between the tipis. He sat up as the Indian neared.

"Good morning, Co-dee," the old man greeted him as he took a seat beside Cody's bed. "Rest well?"

"Yes, sir. Thanks. And thank you kindly for patchin' me up," he said, indicating the bandage over his shoulder. "How bad is this one?"

The Indian frowned, deepening the seams in his coppery face. "Ball pass through. Good."

"Where're my clothes? I need my gear."

"Give to Basket Making Woman. She keep safe."

"Can you get them? I need to get goin'."

"You not lose bad men."

Puzzled, Cody wrinkled his nose. If he didn't get after Murphy and his bunch soon he would never catch up to them.

"I must go after them," Cody insisted.

"Standing Bear go. He keep watch till you ride."

At first Cody didn't understand. Then it dawned on him what Red Eagle had said. Standing Bear had gone after Murphy and his bandits.

"Does he know where they are?"

Red Eagle smiled. "He knows. We all know. He left last night to follow."

Well, at least he hadn't lost them. But if he expected to catch up to them again he had to get on his feet and find out how much his injuries had affected him.

"I need my clothes," Cody said. "I need to move around."

Red Eagle understood. He rose and with easy strides crossed the clearing to one of the other tipis. He bent slightly toward the door flap and called out in his own tongue. A moment later the skin opened and a small woman wearing a plain elkskin dress stepped outside. Her long ebony hair reached past her waist, shimmering in the early morning sunlight. She lifted her wide-spaced, deep brown eyes to Red Eagle. They spoke briefly, then she disappeared into the dwelling, reemerging shortly with a bundle that she handed to Red Eagle. Cody recognized his hat.

As soon as Red Eagle handed the bundle to him, Bailey found his buckskin trousers and stood to pull them on. Struggling with the pants caused his shoulder to start throbbing, and by the time he had buttoned them he felt lightheaded. He sat down on the buffalo hide. Pulling up his knees, he folded his arms on them and laid his head on his forearms. He hadn't expected such weakness and it concerned him. If he'd expended this much energy simply pulling on his britches he was in for a rough time.

He looked up to see the Indian woman coming toward him, carrying his boots in one hand and his pistols by their barrels in the other. Around her neck she wore his powder horn and the bag that held his caps and lead. She had braided her hair with rawhide strips, and a thin belt decorated with seed beads encircled her waist. She walked right up to him, her face expressionless as she lay his boots and firearms on the buffalo robe. Without a word she turned and, as Cody watched, started back to her tipi.

When Basket Making Woman had reentered her tipi, Cody busied himself pulling on the rest of his clothes. A large bloodstain darkened the left front and back of his faded red cotton shirt. The holes where the bullet had entered and exited had been neatly sewn closed with threadlike strands of rawhide. Cody slipped his arms into the sleeves, then rolled them up past his elbows. Finally he tugged on his boots, stamping his feet into them. Once again he rose to his feet. His knees quivered like those of a newborn calf. He realized he was breathing heavily and the ground around him was beginning to reel.

Red Eagle stood close behind him, ready to catch him if he should fall. Cody steadied himself as he struggled to breathe deeply and evenly. He didn't dare attempt to take a step until his head stopped swimming.

"Sit down?"

Cody shook his head.

"I'm all right, so far."

He glanced down at the brace of Colts laying on the blanket, but didn't figure it would be a good idea to reach down and retrieve them. He had no desire to fall on his face like a toddler, even if he did feel like one.

Red Eagle saw Cody eyeing his guns and picked them up, handing them to the Pony rider.

"Thanks," Cody said as he slid the guns into his sash.

Cody had never been shot before, so therefore had nothing by which to gauge the seriousness of his wound. His stained shirt provided mute testimony of his blood loss, along with his unsteadiness. As his dizziness finally began to subside, his stomach commenced rolling.

"I gotta sit down."

Red Eagle guided him to a backrest made of willow rods, supported by a tripod of larger sticks. Cody lay against it as he closed his eyes. One thing he knew now, he wasn't going anywhere today. He only hoped Standing Bear stayed on Murphy's trail until he could catch up.

John Butler had stayed at Elkhorn until daylight, when he had saddled up again to go after Cody. He had stuffed two sacks with some bacon and coffee, jerked beef, and a few cans of beans. He secured the sacks with a length of rope, then threw them behind the cantle like saddlebags. He stepped into the stirrup and hauled himself onto the tall chestnut gelding.

By midmorning he came upon the outlaws' tracks. With his limited tracking skills he failed to find any sign of Cody, but he stayed on this trail. He knew Cody would be following it too. As the sun arched across the sky John urged the chestnut forward at a trot. The tracks left by the bandits had changed, indicating they had slowed down, and John saw a chance to close the gap between himself and Cody.

Less than two hours later he spotted the buzzards circling over the plain. He swallowed hard as he put the spurs to the gelding. With its hoofs pounding the prairie, the chestnut sailed across the level.

John reined the animal to a halt on the bank above the arroyo where Cody had faced the three outlaws. He saw them sprawled in the bed of the wash, the buzzards already making a feast of their carcasses. John leapt into the gap, hissing at the vultures and slapping them away from the dead men with his hat. The birds had done their work, mutilating the bodies, but John saw that Cody wasn't there.

He walked along the arroyo, searching for any sign of Cody, and finally discovered the horseshoe prints near the dead cottonwood root. He studied the situation. Three men dead and the sign indicated a fourth had ridden out. He didn't see any evidence of other horses in the sandy soil. He squinted as he traced the horse's path along the arroyo bottom, until the tracks broke out of the cut and headed eastward. John clambered up the bank onto the bench, staring toward the eastern horizon. A look of puzzlement furrowed his brow as he surveyed the prairie ahead of him. He turned back to the wash and slid over the edge, headed for his horse on the opposite side.

Leading his horse by its reins, John made a quick survey of the outlaws' deserted campsite. His search revealed they had continued south. He turned his eyes to the east again, as he stroked the chestnut's nose.

"Well, boy," he said to the animal. "I guess we're headin' that way."

He swung into the saddle and rode the gelding along the arroyo until he came to a good crossing, then picked up Cody's trail.

The late-afternoon sun had begun to warm John's back when he spied the dark splashes of blood on the brown grass. He brought the red horse to an abrupt halt and vaulted from the saddle. He sat on his haunches as he plucked a blade of the stained grass. He rolled it between his fingers, carefully inspecting it, as he pushed his hat back on his head.

It didn't take anything long to dry out in the broiling sun, so the only information John gleaned from his discovery was that Cody was badly wounded. He rose to his feet and began to examine the terrain, then suddenly froze in midstep. A deep groan rolled from the back of his throat.

There, plain as a crow perched on a snowdrift, was the print of an unshod pony. He circled the patch of blood-stained grass searching for the trail that led from this place. He found two sets of tracks. The unshod pony walked ahead of the horse John had been tracking, indicating the second horse was now being led.

He remounted his horse and started off, riding until the light began to fade and he could no longer see the faint hoofprints. Stopping for the night, he made camp, building a fire from dried buffalo dung. He opened a can of beans with his pocket knife and warmed them near the fire. As the fire blazed before him, John chewed thoughtfully. Once he noticed the chestnut prick up his ears and stare into the darkness, prompting him to draw his gun, but he didn't see or hear anything. When the horse returned to cropping grass, John laid his pistol in his lap, unaware of the Indian who had spied on him.

# CHAPTER 19

STANDING Bear saw the campfire as he retraced the trail to where he had found Cody. Whoever had built the fire had done so right in the middle of the path. The young Indian left his pony and crept toward the encampment, moving as soundlessly as a prowling cat.

He spotted the lone man sitting beside the fire eating. He scoured the darkness at the edges of the firelight, but saw no one else, nor any other horses. When he saw that the tall red horse sensed his presence, alerting the stranger, Standing Bear retreated into the night. He had other business to take care of for Cody, so he wouldn't challenge this interloper who would be no threat to the large encampment of Sioux who had taken the Pony rider into their care.

Standing Bear seized his horse's mane and swung onto its back. He rode until the campfire behind him flickered in the distance like the light of a firefly, then made his own camp.

Big Joe Murphy sat alone, staring into the orange and gray coals of his dying campfire. Once in a while he cast a glance at the girl tending Charillo. He had ordered her to look after the Indian after the raid on the Pony station. It wasn't that he cared all that much about the Comanche—if he had heeded his own instincts he would have left Charillo behind—but his men had demanded the Indian be taken along. And not just a few of them either: their mutiny had been unanimous. Even Ike had stood with them. The rebellion had left Murphy flabbergasted, to the

150

point where he had made no attempt to reassert his command of the gang until this morning, when he had dispatched Harve, Jayce, and Clay to check their backtrail. He had noticed they were the ringleaders of the insurrection and hoped to rid himself of at least one of them by isolating them from the rest of the band. The plan had worked beyond his expectations. They had left all three of them dead in a gully a day's ride north of there, and everything indicated there had been only one gunman.

He had listened to the murmuring as they had continued on their trek to the ford on the Republican. Once he thought he overheard one of the men say something about grabbing the girl for themselves if Charillo died. Murphy had smiled at that. Such talk meant they were getting full of themselves, and Murphy knew how to take advantage of their cockiness and use it against them.

With Charillo out of action, Big Joe had nine able-bodied men. In order for him to regain control he needed to reduce that number before he would be ready to face down the remaining rebels. The thought of leaving this bunch and starting over never occurred to him. It had become a matter of pride. They had humiliated him with their revolt and he couldn't let that pass.

"Hey, Ike? Got a minute?"

Ike left his seat near one of the other fires and sauntered over to where Murphy sat tossing another buffalo chip onto the bed of coals. "Yeah?"

Big Joe lifted his eyes. "Geez, Ike, sit down. Let's have a smoke."

Ike squatted on the opposite side of the fire as Murphy fished in his pockets for his sack of tobacco and pipe. He filled the bowl, then tossed the pouch over the flames to Ike, who did likewise.

"Reckon we'll reach the river tomorrow," Murphy observed.

Ike nodded as he puffed on the chewed stem of his pipe.

"Yes, sir, makin' good time," Big Joe continued. "Why, at this rate we'll be in Texas within a coupla weeks."

"Be good to be home."

"Yep, we might be able to take advantage of this North and South situation and make some real money."

Ike said nothing. He and some of the others had discussed breaking away from Murphy and going it on their own. They had chafed long enough under his tightfisted control and they wanted a change. Some of the older ones, who had ridden with Big Joe since the days of the forty-niners, exhibited a greater reluctance to desert Murphy. They still remembered the big hauls, though the passage of time had embellished their recollections.

Ike favored splitting from Big Joe, but the presence of the emigrant girl complicated things. Several of the men advocated stealing her for their own pleasure, while others wanted nothing to do with her, seeing her as more trouble than they needed right now. Ike had suggested they persuade Murphy to free her, but no one really believed that was even a remote possibility. Someone else recommended killing her outright, but these men, accustomed as they were to violence, shrank from such a singular act. All of the killings they had participated in to this point had been of a distinctly impersonal nature and every man had joined in. It wouldn't take all of them to slay Jenny Rutheford and no man wanted to hold the gun that murdered her. And so the stalemate had developed, stunting the rebellion against Murphy.

"Ain't very talkative this evenin', Ike?"

He shrugged. "You're the one called me over."

Murphy bristled, but held his temper. He had to come up with a plan to make Ike pay for his betrayal. "I did, at that. I wanted to know the mood of the men."

Ike stared into the hungry flames that licked greedily at

the fresh fuel Murphy had thrown on the fire. For a moment Big Joe wondered if Ike had heard him and started to ask his question again. Then Ike responded.

"Ain't much to say. Most of 'em's anxious to get home and get shut of that girl. She ain't been nothin' but trouble."

"Charillo needs her right now."

"He wouldn't have needed her if we hadn't gone back after her."

Murphy clenched his teeth. "What was I supposed to do, Ike? Leave her back there to tell ever'body and their brother about us?"

Ike's eyes narrowed as he peered at Murphy through the flames.

"Don't you think she already told them Pony Express folk? Who do ya think that was followed us and killed Jayce and Clay and Harve?"

"We can outrun a few do-gooders better than a full-fledged posse."

"Well, I hope so," Ike grumbled. "It's gettin' to where there ain't too many of us."

"Zeke and the others will be catching up with us 'fore long," Murphy said, referring to the group he had sent after Crig Rogers and Emory Tatum.

"Reckon they will . . . if they can."

"Ya know, Ike," he said, thrusting the stem of his pipe toward Ike. "You're gettin' downright worrisome."

"How's that?"

"If I was to listen to you, nothin' is gonna turn out."

"Well, you just look at how things've gone the last few days," Ike said as he stood. "Count how many men we started with that ain't here now, how little money we're takin' back with us. Then tell me why I should think anything's gonna come out right? If ya ask me, it seems that old Mexican charm you been wearin' around your neck all these years has lost its magic."

Murphy clenched his fists so tightly his fingernails cut into his palms. It took every ounce of self-control he could muster to keep from lunging over the fire and throttling Ike. All the years they had spent together meant nothing. He knew Ike had deserted him like all the rest.

"I think I'm gonna go along over here, Joe," Ike said, nodding at the fire where he had sat before joining Murphy.

"Yeah," Murphy growled. "Go right ahead."

The steely gray eyes narrowed as they flashed at Ike's retreating back. The outlaw leader decided on a possible method for ridding himself of Ike Pappas. He needed someone to ride the backtrail, to make sure no one followed, and Ike had the experience for that kind of assignment.

He turned the bowl of his pipe upside down, tapping it against the open palm of his left hand to dislodge the ashes. He tucked the worn tobacco furnace into his pocket as he rose and started for his bedroll. He lowered himself onto the blankets, resting his head on his saddle. A few feet away he saw Ike jawing with his cronies around their fire.

Yes, sir. The best way to deal with a poisonous snake was to cut its head off.

Murphy drew the heavy Walker Colt from its holster and laid it across his stomach. He reached inside his shirt and pulled out the battered old medal, its surface worn almost smooth from the years of handling. Words had once graced its front, but they had vanished long ago. All Big Joe could remember of them now was that they had said something about victory. He closed his hand around it, giving a last glance at Jenny's still figure sleeping in the shadows at the edge of his campfire. Once the Indian died, and this business about who ran things was straightened out, he would see to her. No matter what the rest of the men had in mind for Jenny Rutheford, Big Joe knew what he intended to do with her. And so were his thoughts as he drifted off to sleep.

At the first light of dawn Big Joe rose, ready to put his plan into motion. He waited until everyone had eaten and started breaking camp before calling Ike over.

"Yeah, Joe?"

"I'm thinkin' Zeke and his boys oughta be headed our way any time now. I want you to take a ride along our backtrail. Poke around some. Take a man with ya if ya want, but look sharp. If anybody's on our trail I want ya to see them first."

"All right. I'll take Luke Hanson with me. As soon as we're saddled we'll ride out."

A few moments later Ike and Luke trotted their horses northward. Murphy watched impassively as they rode away. He turned to see the eyes of the other men upon him. He figured he would have to kill one of these men to prove just who was leading this outfit, but then everyone else should fall into line until Ike returned. Big Joe smiled to himself. If Ike ever returned.

"Couple ya fellas best help that girl get Charillo loaded on that travois so's we can be on our way."

He was careful not to order anyone to attend to the task. Instead, he let them decide among themselves. The time would come for him to give a direct order, then he would find out who among them thought he was the strongest. Once he had dealt with that man he could leave Charillo behind. Up until now, the gang had moved slowly in an effort to keep the Indian as comfortable as possible, a foolish notion to Big Joe. He knew they had covered less than half of the ground they should have.

At midday Ike and Luke dismounted to stretch their legs and have a bite to eat. They loosened the saddle cinches and picketed their horses at the eastern base of a low hill, then Luke broke out some jerked beef while Ike hunted in his saddlebags until he found some hardtack. They reclined below the hilltop, leisurely munching their food as they watched the towering clouds sail across the sky.

"Gonna be good to get back to Texas," Luke mused.

"I reckon."

"First thing, I'm headin' for San Antone and a week of riotous livin'. I know a few girls down there that'll be right glad to see me."

A smile broke across Ike's sharp features.

"I'll just be glad to get outa this stinkin' place. It ain't brought us much of nothin' but bad luck."

"Brogan says he's ready to take on ol' Joe an be done with him. Swears the quicker we get rid of him the safer we'll all be."

Ike shook his head.

"Don't know as I'd agree with that. Country we're in right now, we may need every man."

"Then why does Murphy keep whittlin' away at us? Sends Chester off after some soldier we could've beat out of the country before he got to the army, then has Zeke and them boys chasin' after a coupla Pony riders. And me and you. Sittin' out here in the middle of nowhere, lookin' for what? Lookin' for who?"

Ike bit off a chaw of jerky, then chewed it thoughtfully.

"I wonder."

"What's that?" Luke asked.

"What's the real reason Joe sent us out here?"

Luke pulled out the cork on his canteen and tipped it to his lips, taking a long gulp. He lowered it, then wiped his mouth on his sleeve. "Thought ya said he wanted us to check our backtrail."

"All you said about Chester and Zeke makes me wonder . . ."

Luke's eyes widened and his mouth gaped. "Ya don't suppose he sent us out here"—he swallowed hard—"to get rid of us?"

"I don't wanna believe it, but the way old Murphy's been actin', ya can't be too sure."

"Well, I'll swan. What're we gonna do?"

"Head back. We've come far enough to see there ain't nobody on our trail. And I say we get goin'."

They scurried down the hill to their horses and swiftly prepared to leave. It was Luke who saw the Indians first. He had his foot in the stirrup and one hand on the horn and the other on the cantle. He gaped at them across the saddle.

"Ike!" he hissed.

"What—"

Then Ike saw them, too. "Take it easy, Luke. Chances are, they just want our horses."

"We'd be dead men without our horses. 'Sides, looks like these boys are painted for war."

Ike could see the paint on their faces without Luke pointing it out.

"We ain't got a lot a choices here. We stand, we die. We run, we die."

The Indians stared stoically as they sat astride their horses.

"I say we make a break for it," Luke said.

"Don't look to be nothin' else we can do," Ike agreed as he stepped into the stirrup. "Let's go," he whispered as he slapped his horse across its hip.

Ike's horse bolted up the hill with him clinging to the horn and cantle while he flattened himself against the near side, unwilling to throw his leg over the saddle. He heard Luke holler indiscernibly behind him, but he didn't look back.

The first arrow struck Ike between the shoulder blades as he hauled himself up into the saddle. It set him up for the next volley, and this time one of the missiles pierced his ribs, toppling him from his horse. He stared at the limitless sky above him, his fingers exploring the wound where the arrowhead had broken through his chest. He felt the ground quake beneath him as the savages approached. A moment later they had gathered around him, their faces silhouetted by the noon sun. He tried to speak, but no words would come.

Standing Bear approached the small Cheyenne war party without trepidation. They were known to him, as he was to them, through the loose alliance of the Sioux and Cheyenne nations. They invited him into their camp, and as the men sat around the cheerfully burning campfire, the Cheyenne soldiers related their encounter with the two white men earlier in the day, using the wide gestures and hand signals of the Plains sign language. They provided the two scalps as evidence of their coups, as well as the shod horses. The warriors had started after a small Pawnee raiding party that had stolen Cheyenne horses, but had happened upon the white men while tracking the horse thieves.

Standing Bear asked if they had seen any other sign of whites.

The leader of the small party nodded, then indicated they had crossed the trail of a band of about ten whites headed south. The Cheyenne hadn't given chase, continuing to pursue their own stolen animals.

The Sioux brave informed his Cheyenne allies that a white man might follow after him, probably riding a horse carrying the *XP* brand of the Pony riders. He described Cody to them and gave them his name and asked them to let him pass in peace.

Only animals of high quality received the *XP* brand, a fact the Cheyenne knew well. Such a horse enhanced the wealth of the brave that possessed it. For that reason some of the Indians didn't want to honor Standing Bear's request. After a few minutes' arguing back and forth, however, they consented to respect their friend's appeal.

The following morning Standing Bear and the war party continued on their separate journeys, but not before the Sioux brave gently reminded his comrades of their pledge not to molest Cody.

# CHAPTER 20

JOHN Butler had followed the tracks of Cody's horse until he finally reached the encampment of the Sioux band led by Red Eagle. He cautiously circled the ring of tipis, searching for any sign of Cody. Then he spied his comrade, walking unsteadily beside a young Indian woman as he clung to her shoulder for support.

Stretching out in the grass, John scrutinized the scene before him. Cody didn't appear to be in any immediate danger from his Indian hosts. John had started to retreat from the edge of the camp when a sudden prick in his back halted him. Slowly he turned over and found himself looking up the shaft of a lance into the stern faces of three Indian boys, not one of them more than ten years old. They motioned for him to rise and he dutifully obeyed.

A broad smile spread over Cody's face when he spied John entering the camp at the point of the youngsters' lances.

"Indian fightin', John?"

He shrugged. "They caught me with my back turned. Friend of yours?" he asked, nodding toward the young woman at Cody's side.

"This is Basket Making Woman."

"Howdy, miss," John said as he tipped his hat.

"This is John," Cody said, clapping his friend on the shoulder.

Basket Making Woman smiled and bowed her head slightly. She then turned to Cody.

"John friend?"

"Yes."

She spoke to the boys, and with obvious reluctance they lowered their spears.

"You hurt bad?"

Cody shook his head. "Don't think so. Basket Making Woman has patched me up pretty good here and she's been helpin' me get my legs back under me again."

"How soon can you ride?"

"I dunno. I'm still kinda woozy, but I might be ready to give it a shot tomorrow."

"Them boys are gettin' a good lead on us. Maybe I oughta go ahead and you can catch up with me later."

"We already got some help there. One of the braves has already gone out to pick up their trail."

Cody lowered his head to Basket Making Woman. "I would like to sit down, please."

"Yes, sit," she replied and led him to the willow backrest beside his buffalo robe bed. She helped him ease himself to the ground, then left the two white men alone.

"What about Boz and the rest of 'em?"

"I don't know about Boz. If he ain't with Murphy and the girl, then I expect we'll find his bones in the ashes of the Freemont Springs station. I caught up with Crig and Emory east of Elkhorn where some of Murphy's men had 'em pinned down. We managed to get out of that and I left Crig and Emory at Freemont and come lookin' for you."

"How was Crig?"

"Still alive when I left 'em, but I don't know how. He was in real bad shape."

Cody knew he had to get back into the saddle and after Murphy. If he let the outlaw escape with Jenny, then his friends would have suffered for nothing. And he had no intention of letting that happen. Now that John had arrived he had someone to ride along with him and help make sure he stayed in the saddle. Concern about his weakness was the only thing that had kept him in the Sioux camp today, as he had feared passing out while pursuing the outlaws, thereby losing them and perhaps his own life.

"It's good to see you, Johnny."

"You too. When I came across the prints of that unshod pony out there I figured you's a goner for sure."

"Naw. These folks been takin' real good care of me."

John surveyed the circle of tipis about them.

"So, what's the story here, Cody? How come they didn't lift your hair?"

Cody related the story of his meeting with Standing Bear a few months before, when he had discovered the Indian afoot on the prairie and had returned him to his people.

"He was the one that found me and brought me here."

"Lucky for you."

The next morning, after Red Eagle and Basket Making Woman had bid them farewell, Cody and John rode out of the Indian camp, heading southwest. It didn't take long for them to pick up the outlaws' trail.

"Still have their wounded man with them," Cody said, squatting in the dust as he inspected the ruts left by the travois. "Looks like they passed through here a couple days ago, movin' pretty slow."

He lifted his eyes and studied the distant horizon.

"I'd say they're headed for the Republican. Probably on their way back to Texas."

"How long you figure on followin' 'em?"

Cody rose and faced John, who stood beside him.

"Till we catch 'em."

"Then what? I'd say they outnumber us pretty good."

Cody nodded.

"That they do. I'd reckon the odds are about five to one."

"So, what've you got in mind?"

"Nothin' yet."

He looked away briefly, then his gaze returned to Butler. "You goin' on with me?"

"Are you kiddin'? After what these guys have done? Why I wouldn't want to miss the fireworks for nothin'," he said, slapping the butt of his holstered revolver. "You oughta know I ain't one to go dodgin' a fight."

"Reckon we best get on the road then."

Cody figured he and John could close the gap between themselves and Murphy's crew before the outlaws reached the Republican River; they had a wounded man slowing them down.

"I think we oughta push our horses a mite harder," Cody said as he swung into the saddle. "We know the general direction these galoots are headed, so I say we make us some time."

"No argument from me."

The sun rose high, roasting their shoulders beneath the cotton shirts stretched across their backs. The land stretched out wide before them, gently rolling away like a calm sea, concealing arroyos and plateaus within its beguiling waves. They rode over the dry prairie, conscious of the dust the horses kicked up.

As the horses trotted over the plain, Cody began to wonder what had become of Standing Bear. He doubted the Indian had given up his chase, but he hadn't seen any sign of him anywhere. Of course Cody's primary concern was keeping focused on the outlaws' trail. Once he found them he didn't figure Standing Bear would be far away.

The sun had been set nearly two hours before Cody and John stopped to make camp. John built a fire of dried buffalo chips while Cody readied a pot of coffee and opened a tin of beans. They ate quietly, listening to the night sounds of the prairie, the coyote calls, the chirping crickets, and once in a while the screech of an owl. Somewhere far away to the west thunder rolled.

Cody watched the stars as they glittered against the

black velvet sky. He remembered that afternoon in Wilkes's store when he had seen Murphy searching through the glass for Jenny. The memory had haunted him ever since he had come to in Red Eagle's camp two nights before. He tried to block out the horrors his imagination conjured up, though when he let himself think about it, he feared the worst had befallen Jenny. He didn't delude himself either, knowing full well the outlaws might already have murdered her. That knowledge only strengthened his resolve to track them down and, if possible, bring them to justice. Not only for Jenny, but for her folks and the countless others whose lives and dreams Murphy and his cutthroats had stolen. He had no one to back him except John. Maybe some of the Express people from Elkhorn might be on their way, but Cody doubted if they would arrive in time to make any difference, and he couldn't wait.

Perhaps his Sioux friend might stand with him, but Cody knew he had no reason to expect that. Whatever debt Standing Bear imagined he owed Cody he had more than repaid already.

Cody glanced at John and saw the stockman stretched out on his bedroll, his head resting on his saddle, hat pulled down over his face. He had seen John working with his six gun many times, doing trick shots, like throwing two silver dollars into the air and shooting both before they hit the ground. Cody had never seen anyone faster, but he didn't know if John had ever fought in a gun battle. The occasion had never arisen to discuss such things, until now.

"You awake?"

John removed his hat, dropping it onto his chest. "Yep."

"You think you're ready to die?"

John smiled at him. "You callin' me out, Cody?"

Cody chuckled. "Reckon a shootout between us would

be pretty close, but I was talkin' about facin' this bunch we're trailin'."

John shrugged. "If my time's up, it's up. I'll tell you one thing, we'll give these boys a run for their money."

"Guess I've had my share of scrapes right along, but I never killed another white man until just a few days ago."

John sat up on his blanket. He plucked a blade of grass, twisting it between his thumb and forefinger. "I had a job as stockman back up the line at Spring Ranch about a year ago—"

Even before John began his story, Cody knew it, and felt foolish that he hadn't recognized John's name before now.

"—I got mixed up in a little fracas between a rancher and the stationmaster about who controlled the road. Well, I was determined to stay out of it and just do my job until this fella shows up at the station with four others, threatening Dave Garth, the company's man. I wasn't about to stand by and see Dave go down alone, so I stepped in."

"I know the story," Cody said. "I think every rider and stockman on the line knows it. Dave Garth said you killed two of 'em and wounded another before he blew one out of the saddle with his shotgun. I recollect readin' a paper where Garth said you had to be the fastest man alive."

John shook his head slowly and threw down the twisted sliver of grass.

"Hmmph! Fastest man alive! It was a dark night and two of 'em were drunk. For all I know they probably all were. Garth was just makin' fool's talk. Why, the two scoundrels that survived that fight never told their side of it. Leastways not that I ever heard. I just hope folks forget about it."

Cody smiled. "I never thought I'd be ridin' into a gunfight with Lightnin' John Butler. Wasn't that what they called you?"

The Pony rider thought he detected a pained expression flit across John's face, but it was quickly replaced by a weak grin. "Let's just keep it 'John' between you and me. Eh, Cody?"

"Well, sure. I didn't mean nothin'—"

"I know. It's just that the first few months after that business I couldn't seem to go anywhere without somebody wantin' to buy me a drink, or draw against me. That's why Garth wrote to Silas and asked if I could come to work out here. So far I ain't had no problems. It's been nice and quiet and that's just the way I like it."

John lay back on his bedroll. "I just hope it stays that way."

Cody stared into the fire until nothing remained of it but radiant embers, thinking how they had followed the outlaws' trail until the stars had shown in the sky. It was obvious to them that the wounded man, whom they both believed was Murphy's Indian scout, had slowed down the bandits' flight. Enough so that Cody expected to intercept them by sundown tomorrow.

He had no thirst for the battle that he knew must come. He didn't remember when the realization had hit him, but for some time now he had known he must face Murphy. When that happened he knew he had but one choice, to kill the errant pilot.

When dawn broke, Cody awakened and found John had already built a fire and had coffee boiling and bacon frying. They ate quickly, both of them anxious to get on the trail.

Cody saddled the buckskin, wishing it were Champion he had under him. When Murphy's bunch torched the station, they had run off all the stock. And even though Cody thought he had seen the mustang's familiar shoe print among those he followed, he wasn't certain. He only hoped the mustang had gotten back to Bonner's station and hadn't ended up on some Indian's string.

He stepped into the stirrup and hoisted himself into the saddle. Although the sun was hardly risen, the day already felt warm and sticky. Cody peered at the hazy curtain that rose like steam over the distant horizon and knew it portended a miserable day. He touched his spurs to the buckskin. John followed suit and they started south once again.

Hardly an hour had passed when they happened onto a flock of feasting buzzards. Startled, the birds fluttered upward and commenced circling overhead. They discovered the bodies of Ike Pappas and Luke Hanson lying in the early morning sun, mutilated beyond any recognition. That the two men had been scalped was readily apparent, but their bodies had also been torn and savaged by the wild beasts of the prairie. The remains that Cody and John found hardly resembled anything human.

"What do you make of it?"

Cody studied the bodies from the buckskin's back, then surveyed the surrounding countryside. "I dunno," he said.

He dismounted and began a careful examination of the area around the corpses. "My guess is they've been dead a day, maybe two. Certainly no more, there's too much of 'em left."

"Indians?"

"Looks like. I'd say they headed east from here," Cody said, pointing at hoofprints in the dust, then to the eastern horizon. "And I see more than a coupla shoe tracks."

John nodded. "Killed for their horses, then?"

"Yep," Cody replied as he remounted the buckskin.

"We ain't gonna bury them?"

Cody shook his head. "No time."

# CHAPTER 21

THE stifling heat of the early afternoon sun and loss of blood had thrown Charillo into a fit of delirium, bringing the gang to a halt. They sat around playing cards while Jenny tended the wounded Indian, but none of her ministrations brought him any relief. Finally, after nearly three hours of Charillo wavering between lucidity and incoherence, Murphy had had enough.

"Get on your horse, girlie! Ever'body! Let's get mounted!"

Jenny looked up from bathing Charillo's brow at the menacing hulk towering over her. She saw he had directed his gaze at the others and not at her.

The men exchanged vaguely puzzled looks.

"C'mon!" Murphy bellowed. "We can't sit around here all day waitin' for this Injun to die. We gotta get movin'!"

No one stirred.

Big Joe wheeled on Jenny.

"All right you, we're pullin' out." With that, he reached down and clamped his beefy fingers around her slender wrist. He squeezed so tightly that Jenny cried out. Her whimper brought one of the men to his feet.

Murphy smiled as he realized he had drawn out the man he sought, the backbone of the remaining rebels. He was one of the men Ike had brought into the gang recently.

"Let her go, Murphy," Frank Brogan growled.

"Why, shore, Frank," Murphy said, releasing Jenny.

She clutched her tattered skirt and scrambled away from the pilot.

"Reckon you're right about that Injun there. He's done beyond helpin'. But now that girl—" Brogan shrugged.

"So, y'all figure to leave old Charillo here and have the girl to yourselves. Is that it?"

"Somethin' like that."

"And just where do I fit into all this?" Murphy asked, letting his eyes soak in the scene before him.

Brogan stood squarely between Big Joe and the other six men. Without taking his eyes off Brogan, Murphy was still able to see that the men behind him hadn't moved yet. That was good. He made his next move.

"The rest of you boys best clear outa there. I wouldn't want any of ya to take a stray slug."

The men traded swift glances, then scurried from behind Brogan. Their departure, however, had no visible effect on Murphy's adversary. His eyes stayed riveted on Big Joe.

As the two men faced each other, Murphy saw something in Frank Brogan's eyes that he didn't like. It wasn't the fiery look of rebellion, or hatred, but the cold look of a killer. Unlike those who had fomented the revolt, Brogan didn't swagger or blow a lot of wind about his toughness. Big Joe wondered why he hadn't shown his hand before. Then it occurred to him that Brogan had waited to make his move when he thought he had the best chance of succeeding. Murphy carefully studied the man standing less than twenty feet from him and knew he confronted a serious challenge.

"I'll tell you where you fit into all this," Brogan said with obvious contempt. "Nowhere."

Murphy didn't flinch, his stare locked on Brogan. He judged his opponent was a good fifteen or twenty years younger than himself. He probably had quicker reflexes and Big Joe figured that perhaps this made Brogan overly confident.

More than ever before, Murphy was conscious of the

ponderousness of the Walker Colt in the holster on his right hip. He had worn it for many years, using it as much for intimidation as for its killing power. But he recognized that Brogan wasn't a man who frightened easily. This situation demanded resolution by death. Murphy decided to bluff Brogan into believing he intended to leave.

A slight smile appeared through the brush covering the gang leader's face.

"All right, Brogan," Murphy said, holding his hands away from his sides. "If that's the way ya wanna have it. Take the girl. Do what ya want with her. Me? I'm gettin' outa here and headin' back to Texas."

He started to turn away.

"Not so fast, Murphy."

The heavy brows knitted and the smile faded as the gray eyes settled once again on Frank Brogan.

"I thought ya wanted me outa here?" Big Joe groused, unhappy with this turn.

"I don't want you ridin' behind me with a gun."

"Well, a man can't get by without a gun in country like this. I might meet up with Injuns, or the law."

"That ain't my problem," Brogan said coldly. "Now, lift that hogleg outa there," he said, nodding at the Walker Colt. "Real slow and easy like."

"You're serious!"

"Get it out! Now!"

Murphy knew he couldn't miss at this distance. And Frank Brogan was showing himself to be the tenderfoot at this business that he was. He had yet to draw his own gun, an ignorant mistake that gave Murphy the edge as soon as his hand closed around the handle of the revolver.

Brogan seemed to realize his blunder, for the hand that hovered near the butt of his pistol suddenly darted for the gun in the low slung holster on his right thigh. The revolver cleared leather and its barrel came parallel to the ground with startling celerity, but even Brogan's mercurial speed couldn't save him.

The Colt bucked in Murphy's hand, hurtling a massive .44-caliber ball into Frank Brogan's chest. Brogan's own pistol roared, its shot wide, kicking up dust between Murphy and Jenny. Brogan fumbled to cock his revolver again, but another slug plowed into his cheek, rocking him onto his heels. The gun slipped from his fingers as his knees buckled. He crumpled into the dust.

Murphy deliberately holstered his gun, then turned to the others. "Anybody else wanna have a go at me?"

No one spoke.

"All right, then. Let's get goin'."

He spun on his heels and glared at Jenny still cowering near the dying Comanche.

"Nobody to save ya now, girl. Ya best get that settled in your head right now. From here on out, ya do what I tell ya."

Jenny struggled to rise, then turned her back on Charillo and started for Champion. No one moved to help her mount the mustang, no one ever did. Stepping into the stirrup Jenny hauled herself into the saddle. She had clung to Champion ever since her abduction from the Pony station at North Platte as if he provided a lifeline back to the world these murderers had snatched her away from. The gelding dutifully responded to her gentle prodding and fell in line in Murphy's column, a meager remnant of the horde that had fallen upon the emigrant train.

The day grew hotter and the sun crept across the sky at a turtle's pace. Except for Murphy and Jenny, everyone rode as if they had fallen asleep in their saddles, heads down and bobbing as their horses plodded forward.

Jenny's eyes surveyed the rolling prairie and beheld a vast, empty land. She hadn't spoken to anyone during her captivity, not even to the dying Charillo. A heavy layer of grit and grime veiled her beauty and blanketed her clothing. She had tied her hair back with a piece of her petticoat, but several strands hung loosely about her face, heightening her already haggard appearance. Three days of riding in the searing sun had scorched her creamy complexion. But for all of her obvious discomfort, more suffering lay ahead if someone didn't reach her soon.

Cody and John reined their horses to a halt, then dismounted for a closer look at the dead man. He lay face up on the dry, flinty plain, a dark bullet hole in his left cheek and a mass of dried blood on his shirtfront. Cody sat on his haunches beside the body.

"This fella ain't been dead long. He's just startin' to stiffen up." Cody stood. "We're close. I know it."

"Well, I'll tell you one thing. This ain't the man that's been ridin' on that travois," John said, pointing at the crude sled.

Cody nodded. No one had made any attempt to stem the flow of blood from this man's wounds.

"What do ya reckon happened to the fella they were cartin' around?" he asked.

"He got better?"

"Reckon we oughta take a look around."

They searched the ground near the dead man, then fanned out in widening circles, until John spotted a peculiar track.

"Cody! Better come have a look!"

"I found their trail. They're still headin' south," he said as he stepped up beside John. "What've you got?"

"I'd say our man on the travois got left behind, then tried to take off on his own."

The tracks cut a wide swath, as though someone had drug a sack of potatoes through the parched grass.

"Do we go after him?"

Cody shook his head.

"Nope." He pointed south. "We're headed in that direction."

The western horizon was aflame with streaks of annatto and vermilion as the sun dipped to the earth. The heat of the day had begun to wane and a refreshing catspaw streamed across the desert from the northwest, a welcome change from the usual southern breezes that dominated the plains during the summer months. Even in the midst of such a grave task, Cody wasn't oblivious to the welcome break in the weather. Removing his hat, he combed his hair with his fingers.

It was John who spied the Indian riding down on them, mounted on a powerfully built black stallion. He reached for his gun as he called to Cody.

"I hope this is your friend," he said, nodding toward the approaching Indian.

"That's him!"

Standing Bear reined the sturdy horse to a halt before them. He began speaking, using the Plains sign language, a form of communication Cody hadn't mastered, but not foreign to John.

"He says it's good to see you ridin' and that the men we're lookin' for aren't too far ahead. If we ride hard we could reach their camp before dark."

Cody turned in his saddle. "You know sign?"

"I understand most of it. I spent some time with the Pawnee on the Loup River. I had a job with the Indian agent there. Got on pretty well with them folks. Of course, that wouldn't please your friend here."

Indeed, Standing Bear's eyes had narrowed at the white man's mention of the Pawnee. John explained his relationship to the Sioux's enemy, which appeared to set the young Indian at ease; he continued his report.

Standing Bear told them of his encounter with the Cheyenne who had killed Ike and Luke and the incident he had witnessed between Murphy and Frank Brogan. He also related Charillo's fate. The Comanche's former allies had left him behind to die, which he had done after crawling away from the site of the shooting. Standing Bear couldn't say why he had done so.

"Standing Bear says he has to get back to his band 'cause this is Pawnee country."

"I thought the Pawnee lived on their reservation?"

John nodded. "Yeah, but they still have to get out and hunt some to stay alive. They ain't the world's best farmers."

"Tell him I'm greatly indebted to him for seeing to my wounds and keepin' after these varmints."

John relayed Cody's message, then the brave responded.

"He will always remember your kindness, and hopes you'll remember his," John interpreted."He says six men are camped near Red Willow Creek and the girl is with them. He wishes you well and says good-bye."

With that, Standing Bear dug his heels into the black stallion's flanks and galloped north.

"Well, at least Jenny is still alive," John said.

Cody drew one of the Colts from his sash and checked each of the chambers, then replaced it and drew the other, repeating the examination.

He tucked the pistol into the brightly colored cloth that encircled his waist.

"Let's go."

They spurred their horses hard and the animals lunged into a gallop. The gently undulating prairie rose and fell beneath the pounding hoofs as the riders crouched low in their saddles, cold, determined eyes sweeping the plains ahead. They knew where Red Willow Creek ran and of a choice campsite along its banks. Within a couple of hours they expected to overtake Murphy and his men.

# CHAPTER 22

MURPHY ordered two of the men to gather firewood from among the dried stems and branches that had fallen from the sparse trees lining the creek bank, while he watched the other men reel out their bedrolls and set up the camp. He settled down on his own blankets and reclined against his saddle. Digging in his pockets, he pulled out his pipe and tobacco pouch. He loaded the bowl, then lit a match and held it to the shredded leaf, puffing until the tobacco glowed red. He carelessly cast the lucifer aside.

He had achieved what he had desired. He had reclaimed leadership of the gang. He hadn't cared so much for the men—he could always raise another gang. He couldn't stand the thought of others attempting to take from him what he had built up.

Now his thoughts turned to self-preservation and the girl. It concerned him that Zeke and the men sent with him hadn't come back, not even one of them. And what about the gunfight that had left Harve and Jayce and Clay dead back there in that wash? Whoever the gunman was obviously knew how to handle a six-shooter. His bullets had done their work.

Glancing about at the remnants of his band, Murphy concluded the time had come to strike out alone with the girl. If anyone still pursued them, such a move would certainly cause confusion. He knew well the hazards of tramping through this country, but right now figured it was in his best interest to get away from the rest of these men he considered nothing more than squareheads.

His eyes lingered on Jenny, who sat near the pinto

gelding, looking sullenly at the ground, her wrists bound in front of her and resting in her lap. He had noticed before that she seemed to have formed an attachment to the mustang. He didn't really know why, but suddenly her affection for the pony annoyed him. As he stroked his beard he decided the horse must go.

"Hey! Devlin!" he shouted to a dark squat man busily spreading his bedroll.

Devlin left his blankets and waddled toward Murphy, his swarthy face a mask of wariness. "Yeah, Joe?"

"I want you to take that pinto the girl's been ridin'."

Devlin wrinkled his pug nose as he studied the gelding. The mustang looked sturdy and he saw the *XP* brand. Everyone knew that meant quality horseflesh. It certainly beat the crow bait Devlin had ridden since joining Murphy's outfit and he jumped at the offer.

"Saddle go with 'im?"

"Nope. Keep your own."

Devlin shrugged. "All right with me."

The stocky outlaw dragged his heels to where Champion stood picketed, cropping grass. The mustang nickered and shied as Devlin reached for the saddle. The gelding's protest drew Jenny's attention. Her head shot up at the sight of the fat bandit working the cinch. She scrambled to her feet.

"Get your hands off him," she said, her voice laced with anger.

"Go on with ya, girl," Devlin said over his shoulder. "Murphy says me and you are swappin' horses."

The girl wheeled on the pilot.

The delight Big Joe got from taking her horse showed plainly on his face. An evil smile parted his beard, revealing his yellowed teeth, but his gray eyes reflected no humor.

She lunged at the brute, clawing at his face, but Jenny's bound wrists prevented her from inflicting anything more serious than pink welts across his cheekbones. Murphy cursed as he backhanded her with a savage blow upside her head that hurled Jenny to the dust. She lay there, sobbing as she curled into a ball.

"Don't ya try nothin' like that again!" Big Joe roared, pointing a beefy finger at her. "I told ya before, there ain't nobody can help ya now!" He smiled wickedly. "It'd do ya well to be a little nicer to me."

Murphy glanced at Devlin. "Take the horse."

The two men collecting firewood returned to the camp and began a fire. Once the flames began dancing, coffee was put on.

"Well, boys," Murphy said as he sat on his haunches beside the fire and poured himself a cup of coffee. "I figure it's about time we split up."

The men traded puzzled looks.

"Ya mean ya breakin' up the gang?" one of them asked in amazement.

Murphy took a careful sip from the steaming cup.

The men assembled about the campfire had witnessed Big Joe whittle away at his outlaw band over the last several days. When out of their leader's earshot a couple of them had even discussed lighting out after dark this very night. They had seen the depth of Murphy's commitment to his men and didn't want to risk becoming his next victims. Now he had so much as told them to go.

"I ain't sure we're bein' followed," Big Joe began. "But Ike and Luke ain't come back and Zeke and none of the boys with him have come back. So, I say we all take out for Texas on our own. Ever'body rides on alone, except I'll be takin' the girl with me." He studied their faces, waiting for someone to protest, but no one spoke. "Good. Me and the girl are leavin' now. And I want the rest of ya to get goin' real quick too."

With that, Murphy rose from the fire, slinging the dregs of his coffee into the flames. Before he turned away he looked at Devlin. "Put the girl's saddle on that hay burner of yours."

The heavyset bandit nodded as he hustled to his feet.

The pilot sauntered away from the fire, his heels scuffing the sand as he headed for his gear. He hoisted his saddle over his shoulder, hauling it to where he had picketed his horse. He plopped the saddle onto the big roan's back, then gazed over the saddle seat as the men set about breaking the camp they had completed setting up less than an hour before. Murphy was glad to be parting from this bunch. Ike had picked most of them, and except for Frank Brogan and maybe Chester Hailey, most of them had shown hardly any backbone. It never occurred to Big Joe that the very men who had enough gumption to stand up to him were the ones he couldn't tolerate and schemed to get rid of. He had always considered Ike Pappas a friend, though a somewhat mealymouthed one, until the rawboned Texan had sided with those who had challenged him. Consequently Murphy had terminated their friendship.

When everyone had saddled up, Murphy called for them to join him at the side of the smoldering campfire. The men gathered around him as he squatted.

"All right," he said as he picked up a long, dried willow twig and began scratching in the sand. "This is about where we are right now. I want two of ya to head due east for a couple of hours, then break off from each other and ride at least another hour before ya make camp for the night. Two more of ya do the same thing, except I want you to ride out to the southeast. Then I want two of ya to make straight for the ford on the Republican. Ya should get there sometime tomorrow and once ya cross, split up and head for Texas."

Murphy cast aside the twig, then smoothed over the sand where he had drawn before he stood.

"I don't care which of ya goes where. But if ya want to

protect yourselves from gettin' caught I'd recommend ya follow my plan. If there's a posse on our trail, this'll sure confuse 'em some. And in this country they won't be in such an all-fired hurry to break up and head in four different directions."

The others nodded their agreement.

"Good. Well." Murphy sighed as he extended his hand to each one of his remaining subordinates. "We'll surely meet again someday. You boys watch your backs. ¡Adíos!"

They watched Jenny grasp the horn of the saddle on Devlin's old horse and wearily lift her foot into the stirrup. With great effort she swung into the saddle just before Murphy spurred his roan and began leading her horse westward.

Moments later the camp was empty. The outlaws had mounted up as soon as Big Joe had turned west. They followed his plan, splitting into three groups of two men each. Pete Devlin, aboard Champion, rode with Charlie Colby toward the Republican River.

The brilliant scarlet and amber rays of the setting sun pierced the building clouds along the western horizon like polished dagger blades as Murphy drew the roan to a halt on a bench above a small stream with a meager flow of water. He picketed both of the horses in the hip-deep arroyo so they could drink from the creek and still crop the grass that grew on the plain above it. He unsaddled his roan, but didn't move to help Jenny from her horse.

The weary emigrant girl peered at her captor through eyes rimmed red with fatigue and ringed by dark circles. She watched as the massive barbarian hauled his saddle up the embankment and dropped it to the dust. He untied his bedroll from behind the cantle, then spread the blankets on the ground. He turned to Jenny.

"Might as well get on down from there, girl, and lay out your bed," he said, an evil sneer parting his beard as he kicked at the earth next to his own blankets. "Right here by mine."

Jenny swallowed hard, then sucked in a deep breath. "I can't do anything with my hands tied," she said evenly.

Big Joe squinted at her.

"Don't you be gettin' any funny ideas about runnin' off. Out here there ain't nothin' but wolves and Injuns for company. And they ain't near as sociable as I am."

Murphy cut the bindings on Jenny's wrist and left her sitting astride her horse while he clambered back up the slope to where he had started making camp. For a moment she kept her eyes riveted on his back, then she let them slowly survey the barren land about her. She knew nothing of living in the desert. All of her life her folks had pampered her, providing her every need and most of her desires. She hadn't even ridden a horse as much in her entire life as she had these last few days.

Her hands tightened around the saddle horn as she stared into the bleak wilderness. Suddenly, with savage fury, she drove her heels into the horse's ribs. The animal cried out, but nevertheless dutifully responded to her prodding, surging across the stream and bounding up the opposite bank and onto the level.

Big Joe had just flopped onto his blankets, annoyed that Jenny remained on her horse, when he heard her animal's plaintive neighing. He lunged to his feet, swearing and hollering for her to stop. He threw his hat to the ground in disgust as he watched her horse gallop away over the level plain.

When he had warned her about running off he hadn't really believed she would attempt to do so, thinking she didn't have the sand to face the desert alone. Now here it was nigh on to dark and she had taken off across the prairie. As he watched the girl's flight, he mulled over in his mind whether to give chase now or wait until morning. They hadn't pushed the horses hard at all, what with everyone wanting to make traveling easier on Charillo, and that meant she could run her animal hard for a good while. Even if it was Devlin's old crow bait. But Murphy figured the girl would run the horse to ground, being too ignorant to let it rest, and soon find herself afoot. Staring after her, all he could make out now was a cloud of dust.

He bent over and picked up his hat, then clapped it onto his head as he straightened.

"Go ahead and run, girlie. Run hard and fast. I'll still be seein' ya in the mornin'."

Pete Devlin squatted near the fire, cradling his rifle in his lap as he poured himself a cup of coffee. His companion had already turned in and lay in the flickering shadows on the other side of the campfire, snoring softly. They had cut cards to see who took the first watch and Devlin had lost with a deuce.

Behind him he heard one of the horses blow and nicker. He slowly lowered the tin cup, then rose unhurriedly to his feet. This was Pawnee and Arapaho territory, and like other Indians, they were known to steal horses. Devlin slipped away from the firelight into the darkness of the desert. He studied the vague silhouettes of the horses, alert for any peculiarities in their forms, but if there were any discrepancies the night veiled them from his eyes.

He began to circle the camp, heading for the place they had picketed their horses. He took deliberate care with each step he made, trying to move as noiselessly as possible before coming to a halt near the picket line. He licked his lips nervously, then lifted his right foot to move forward. Suddenly he stopped, inhaling sharply as the barrel of a gun pressed hard against his back.

"Don't shoot!" he pleaded.

"Keep your mouth shut and lay the rifle down."

# CHAPTER 23

AT dusk, as dark clouds began gathering in the western sky, Cody and John found the remains of the outlaws' encampment on the bank of Red Willow Creek. Cody sifted through the ashes of the fire and found they were still warm.

"Well, what do you think?" John asked.

"Fire's been out maybe a couple hours," Cody said as he stood, clapping his hands together and checking the position of the sun. "Light's about gone. We better see if we can pick up any sign."

They searched the sandy soil around the camp until they came upon some tracks. And what they found dismayed them.

"They've split up," Cody moaned.

"They sure have," John concurred as he shook his head and began looking for more tracks.

Cody stared dejectedly at the hoofprints in the dust at his feet. As best as he could tell, only two riders had headed west. That left four others to account for. He walked past John to the opposite side of the camp and found the tracks of two more horses that pointed due east. He didn't know why, but he hadn't given any thought to this possibility. Especially now, when the gang appeared so small already. Although he and John never spoke of it, they knew they had engaged themselves in a risky venture pursuing these outlaws. At any moment they might find themselves face to face with marauding Indians, but they had taken on this quest willingly. However, Cody couldn't understand why Murphy had split his gang up now. A call from John interrupted his musings.

"I've got two sets of prints goin' due south! You better have a look!"

Cody strode toward the spot where John crouched, his fingertips tracing the prints he had found. He knelt beside John and saw right away the notched hoofprint John was inspecting so carefully.

"Well, look here."

"I'd say we've hit the jackpot. That's the cleanest print I've seen and I'm sure it's Champ's."

"I wonder," Cody said as he stood. "Even if she ain't with whoever's ridin' Champ, they're gonna know which way Murphy did go."

"Might. We gonna try and track 'em in the dark?"

Cody grinned.

"Won't be much trackin' to it. I imagine if we head south we're gonna find the folks ridin' these horses." A worried look furrowed his brow. "I just wish we could ride a little faster."

"Yeah, take a big chance runnin' these horses in the dark."

"They aren't too far gone. And from the look of those prints I'd say they weren't in too big a hurry." He removed his hat and ran his fingers through his hair like a comb. "We best get after them."

The two men mounted and turned their horses southward.

Stars began to twinkle in the clear skies to the east, but Cody kept a wary eye on the ominous, roiling clouds in the west. Though they appeared to be far away, the speed with which the towering thunderheads tumbled over one another indicated the storm they presaged was moving rapidly toward them. He hoped to overtake the duo ahead of them before it hit. Suddenly a deeper, more gut-wrenching thought occurred to him. If the rain came it would most certainly wash away the sign left by those they hadn't been able to follow. Cody tried to push the idea from his mind.

They spotted the distant light shortly before midnight.

"That's them. It's gotta be."

"Let's ride in a little closer, then we can go in the rest of the way on foot," Cody said. He too believed they had found their quarry, but the memory of Standing Bear's encounter with the Cheyenne was still fresh in his mind and he had no intention of stumbling onto an Indian village, or a band of marauders.

Cody and John rode to within a couple hundred yards of the fire, then dismounted and hobbled the horses. They moved slowly through the dry grass, cautiously approaching the camp before them. When they had closed to within fifty feet, they knew what they had found.

One man lay near the campfire, his hat pulled low over his eyes, his chest rising and falling with the rhythm of sleep. The other man squatted beside the fire with his back to Cody and John. Cody saw the rifle barrel protruding from beneath the man's arm as he reached for the coffeepot next to the fire. Just as the man poured himself a cupful, Cody heard Champion blow and nicker. The man beside the fire froze for only a moment, then slowly rose.

The horses stood picketed less than ten yards to Cody's right, but he kept his eyes fixed on the man with the rifle, who now started edging away from the fire and the horses. The outlaw moved into the darkness, his body framed by the starlit eastern sky, and began moving toward the Expressmen's position. Cody and John never lost sight of him, crouching low as he neared. He took a few tentative steps past them and stopped, as if listening for some telltale noise, but except for the sounds of the prairie, all was quiet.

Once the bandit had moved past, Cody rose stealthily,

drawing one of the Colt Navy's as he stood. He pushed the pistol hard into Pete Devlin's back.

"Don't shoot," Devlin whined.

"Keep your mouth shut and lay the rifle down," Cody ordered.

Devlin complied, letting the Spencer drop at his feet with a thud.

"All right," Cody said. "Let's move over to the fire and wake up your friend. And just move nice and slow."

John drew his revolver as they started for the camp, Devlin in the lead with his hands raised.

"Wake him up," John said, leveling his pistol at Pete.

"Charlie! Wake up and move slow! The law's on us!"

The man lifted his hat warily, peeking from beneath the brim. Seeing Cody and John, he pushed his hat back on his head as he carefully sat up.

"On your feet!" Cody commanded. He prodded Devlin with the Colt's muzzle. "Move on over there with your friend."

"What's goin' on here?" The bleary-eyed outlaw asked. "What's this all about?"

"We're here lookin' for the men who burned out an emigrant train north of here. Murdered everyone. Everyone, that is, except a young girl."

Cody saw the furtive glances the men exchanged.

"So happens they also raided the Pony Express station at Freemont Springs."

"Look here, young fella," Pete Devlin stammered. "We didn't have nothin' to do with anythin' like that."

A wry smile twisted Cody's mouth as he holstered his gun. He cocked his head toward John, without taking his eyes off the bandits. "You hear that?"

"I heard him. I say we just bed 'em down here and now, and get on with huntin' the rest of their pals."

"I'm tellin' ya, you're makin' a big mistake!"

"A mistake?" Cody shook his head wearily as he squatted

by the fire and helped himself to coffee. "Who's ridin' the pinto you got picketed over there? The one wearin' the *XP* brand?"

The bandit who'd had his slumber interrupted turned his eyes on Pete, betraying his comrade.

Sweat popped out on Devlin's forehead when he realized all eyes had turned on him.

"Now hold on," he pleaded. "I bought that horse. Just today."

"You'll be showin' us a bill of sale then," Cody said, standing.

The other outlaw began to edge away from Devlin.

"You just hold your ground," John ordered.

Suddenly Cody came to the realization that he had relieved Devlin of his rifle, but had failed to take his handgun. And at that very moment the chubby outlaw's hand darted for his revolver. The bandit's cohort saw him make his move and scrambled to retrieve his own weapon. There was no contest.

Cody's pistol came into his hand and bucked with a roar. The slug slammed into Devlin's chest, rocking him on his heels. The outlaw's own gun never cleared leather.

John hollered at the other man to halt. He heeded John's warning, raising his hands as he looked at Devlin, who had collapsed in a heap onto his blankets.

"Don't shoot!" the surviving desperado implored them, lifting his hands high above his head.

"Which trail did Murphy take?" Cody demanded.

The outlaw glanced at his fallen friend.

"He'll never tell Murphy," Cody said.

"What happens to me if I tell ya?"

"It's what happens to you if you don't, that you oughta be worried about," John replied, thumbing back the hammer of his revolver.

"He headed west."

"The girl still with him?" Cody asked.

The outlaw nodded. "Last I saw, she was."

"What're we gonna do with this varmint?"

Cody shrugged. "I guess we head back to the place where the trails branch off. You can take him back to the law."

"And you go after Murphy alone?"

"Don't see where we got much choice. Do you?"

"Well, we could just save the law a little time with this skunk," John said, pointing the muzzle of his gun at the outlaw. "And finish him off here."

"Don't kill me!" the man begged. "For God's sake don't kill me! I told ya what ya wanted to know!"

How easy it would be to ride off and leave this man here, dead with his friend. Cody's trigger finger tensed as his thumb hooked the Colt's hammer. There was no question in Cody's mind the man deserved a death sentence. He had murdered men, women, and children without restraint. Then suddenly Cody's hand relaxed. He realized it wasn't in him to kill another in cold blood.

"C'mon, Johnny," Cody said.

"Kinda wonder if any of those emigrants begged for their lives? What do you think, Cody?"

"Why don't you see if you can find somethin' to tie him up with," Cody said. "I'll keep an eye on him."

John eased the hammer down, then holstered his pistol.

"Sure, Cody. I'll bring our horses up, too." John turned away and left the circle of light near the fire.

"Thanks, kid. He'd a killed me for sure. Why, I—"

"Shut up, or maybe I'll call him back here. Now, move away from them blankets."

Once they had bound their prisoner, Cody and John sat cross-legged beside the fire, sipping coffee.

"Well, what's your next move?"

Cody shook his head slowly. "Like I said before, we head back to where the trails branch off and I take after

Murphy while you deliver our package." He hitched his thumb at the dour-faced outlaw.

"Well, maybe Emory got to the law and it won't be too long before a posse catches up with us."

"We can't wait for that."

John grinned.

"I wouldn't even think of suggestin' such a thing. I merely wanted to make you aware there might be some help followin'."

"Even if somebody's comin' along, I reckon it'll all be over one way or the other before they overtake us."

"I suppose so."

Cody peered into the flames as he speculated about what lay ahead. He was certain now that he would have to confront Murphy alone, but that didn't concern him so much. He had pretty much figured it that way since he had ridden out of Freemont Springs after the outlaws. He hoped Jenny was still alive.

They finished their coffee and began the trek back to the outlaw camp where the trails had diverged, with Charlie Colby in tow. Sunup was still another three or four hours away when they reached their destination on the banks of Red Willow Creek. Thunder rumbled deep and low off to the north as they dismounted, but the sky overhead remained clear, glistening with stars. Cody stripped his saddle from the buckskin and transferred it to Champion, grateful to have the fleet mustang in his possession once again.

"I take it you're ridin' on before daylight?"

"Got to make some time. And Champ appears pretty fresh."

"Sure you wanna leave me and ol' Charlie here by ourselves?"

Cody finished pulling the cinch tight before facing John. "Would you really have shot him back there?"

"This is a rough country, Cody. When a man takes to

shootin' at me, I aim to shoot back. Charlie figured to kill us, just like him and his pals murdered them emigrants, but they thought they were quicker than us. One of them paid the price for his ignorance, while Charlie got off lucky."

"That doesn't answer my question."

"Just between me and you, I never shot a man in cold blood. I just wanted to throw a little scare into Charlie."

Cody sighed with relief. He liked John and it had disturbed him to think he had it in him to kill so remorselessly. Cody didn't shrink from violence himself, neither did he seek it. However, many years ago he had come to the conclusion that violence and evil didn't afflict only those who chose to live their lives according to such wickedness, but, as the Good Book said, fell as the rain on the just and the unjust. The measure of a man was how he reacted to it. And Cody knew that sometimes when a man chose to stand against barbarians he risked becoming one himself. He was glad that hadn't happened to John. Or to himself.

He shook hands with John, then leapt onto Champion's back. "Keep your eyes on that yahoo."

"Don't worry about me. You just watch out for Murphy."

# CHAPTER 24

BIG Joe Murphy swallowed two gulps of water from his canteen, then wiped his mouth on his sleeve before driving the cork into the opening of the flask. He had risen well before sunup, after a restless night of sleep, and had saddled the deep-chested roan. He built no fire, as he was anxious to ride after the Rutheford girl. Several times during the night he had heard the rumbling thunder and had feared the storm it heralded would strike, wiping out any trace the girl had left behind, but to his relief it had passed far to the north. He hooked the canteen's strap over the saddle horn, then stepped into the stirrup, hauling himself onto the big roan's back.

He didn't know this land. When he and his men had come up from Texas they had forded the Republican and made for the Platte, intending to make their fortunes along its sandy banks. Murphy had familiarized himself only with the land that lay along the Central Route and hadn't made any effort to reconnoiter any of the desert beyond its course. Of course Charillo had spent a great deal of time learning the land. That had been his principle job, learning the lay of the country in case they had to make an unplanned escape. But Charillo was gone and his knowledge with him.

Murphy wished now that he had ridden after Jenny as soon as she had made her break. For all he knew she might have found her way to some ranch, or farm. Maybe even a settlement of some kind. He actually debated whether or not to give it up and strike out for Texas, but once again he couldn't get the thought of her out of his mind. He had to have her. And then he had to destroy her.

Gathering the reins in his hands he prepared to goad the roan down the low embankment and across the stream.

"Don't move, Murphy!"

The icy coldness in Cody's voice cut through the dank, early morning air like a saber.

"What d'ya want?" Big Joe demanded.

"Where's the girl?"

"I don't know what yer talkin' about. I'm out here alone."

Murphy heard the faint ringing of spurs behind him as his unseen foe approached. "You're alone now, all right. But I've been followin' ya ever since that raid you and your gang made on the Pony station at Freemont Springs."

"You the fella that gunned down three of my boys in a gulley back east of here?" Murphy asked, starting to turn in his saddle.

"You just sit tight," Cody ordered, halting as he cocked his revolver.

"It was you, wasn't it?" Murphy asked, recognizing the distinctive click as Cody drew back the hammer of his gun.

"It was me."

"Well, come around here and let me have a look at ya. Or ya got it in mind to back-shoot me?"

"Hook the reins around the horn, then let your hands drop to your side."

"Whatever ya say. I don't want no trouble."

"Strange thing for a man who's just murdered a whole emigrant train to say."

Big Joe followed Cody's instructions, tying off the reins before dropping his hands.

"What're ya talkin' about? Murder?"

"I'm takin' you back to Parker's Junction. The folks there will decide what to do with you. Maybe they'll turn you over to the army. No matter. However it goes I reckon you'll hang."

Perched rigidly atop the roan, Murphy stared straight ahead. He knew the faceless voice spoke the truth. At one time only the girl might have implicated him, but that had changed. He had gone too far. At this point he had no idea how many people could identify him. What about the two men he and his gang had encountered at the burned-out remains of the train? Charillo had told Murphy he had seen them at the station. So many loose ends. He had never been so careless, and all because of that girl.

Suddenly it occurred to Murphy that Jenny might provide him with an avenue of escape. This fellow who had gotten the drop on him had asked about the girl.

"All right, all right," Murphy said, feigning resignation. "I don't know about this murder you're talkin' about, but I'll tell ya I did have a girl with me."

The spurs sang again as his enemy resumed his approach.

"I'm listenin'."

"Well, I found her wanderin' on the prairie, ya see—"

Cody stepped up beside the roan, the dark muzzle of his Colt pointing at the pilot's head. "Don't bother with any fancy stories, Murphy," Cody said contemptuously. "I already know the truth."

Big Joe couldn't contain his astonishment. "Why, you're that pup I ran into back in that jerkwater town!"

"Parker's Junction was the place. I'm Cody Bailey. And I know what you're all about, Murphy," he said, spitting the pilot's name out scornfully.

"It was you found the girl at the train?"

"After those butchers of yours finished with it."

"Well, boy, look around. Do ya see her here now?" Big Joe asked as his eyes widened.

"I'm listenin'."

"She took off last night. Headed across the creek there

and I ain't seen her since. Ain't no tellin' what she run into out there."

"And you didn't go after her?"

Big Joe shrugged. "Didn't figger on havin' any trouble catchin' up with her today. She probably rode that flea-bitten nag of Devlin's last night till it dropped."

A treacherous grin spread beneath Murphy's beard. "So, what're ya gonna do now, boy? Take me in, or go after her?"

Cody stood in the predawn darkness, his pistol trained on the silhouette of the hulking outlaw, trying to decide what to do. As tough as he believed Jenny was, Cody didn't give her much chance of survival out there in the desert. If the brutal elements of nature didn't spell her demise, the Indians would. Cody knew they took captives, and a light-skinned woman with honey-colored hair would make a great prize. He realized he really had no choice. He couldn't kill Murphy or leave him here, bound and un-armed, prey to whatever, or whoever, came along. And he couldn't let him go. He had no choice but to take him along in his hunt for Jenny.

Cody didn't like the decision he had reached, as it meant getting closer to Murphy than he cared to. He knew he had to handle the matter with extreme caution.

"Looks like you're gonna be comin' along with me, Murphy. I want you to hold your hands over your head. High."

Big Joe complied, the smile on his face hidden by the early morning darkness.

"Pitch your gun out in front of your horse."

The bandit lowered his left hand.

"Hold it! Reckon you better use your right hand. And just two fingers on the gun butt."

"Ya ain't so wet behind the ears, are ya, boy," Murphy said, a trace of surprise in his voice. He pulled the Walker Colt gingerly from its holster, then cast it away as instructed. It landed with a heavy thud in the grass in front of the roan.

"I want you to climb down from there real nice and easy. And keep them hands where I can see 'em."

Big Joe grasped the saddle horn with both hands, then swung his right leg over the cantle. For a brief moment he hung on the near side of the roan, suspended above the ground, his left foot still in the stirrup. Then he slowly began to lower his right foot to the ground. Suddenly, with such force that the roan stumbled, Big Joe turned as he pushed his massive frame off the horse's side and into Cody.

Cody fired his revolver as Murphy leapt at him. The pilot's lunging body crashed into him before Cody knew what became of his shot, or before he could squeeze off another. The collision with Murphy jarred the pistol from his hand and sent him sprawling in the grass.

Murphy rolled onto his right shoulder as he hit the ground, somersaulting to his feet, his back to the Pony rider. The slug from Cody's gun had struck him high on the right side of his chest and blood already soaked the front of his buckskin shirt. He labored to catch his breath even as he turned to attack Cody again. In the darkness he hadn't seen that Cody carried another gun in his sash.

Cody lay flat on his back, his head swimming. He knew he had to get up and move before Big Joe could pounce on him again, but the pilot's lunge had caught him full in the chest, knocking the wind right out of him. He struggled to roll onto his stomach, vaguely aware of a growing light in the east. He crawled onto his hands and knees, gasping for air. Then suddenly Murphy was there beside him. Cody made a vain attempt to dodge the toe of Murphy's boot as it drove into his ribs, once again flipping him onto his back.

"So, ya thought ya could take me in, huh, whelp?" Big

Joe panted. "Ya shouldn't have stuck yer nose in my business, boy. 'Cause I aim to kill ya for it."

Cody had no doubts that Murphy intended to do just that. Clutching his right side and fighting a wave of nausea, he scrambled to his knees in time to see the outlaw, his broad, bearded face a mask of fury, bearing down on him. He tried to duck the punch Big Joe hurled at him and grab the Colt in his sash. He wasn't quick enough, failing to dodge Murphy's swing or secure his gun. He did manage to avoid taking the full force of the jab that otherwise would have rendered him unconscious. However, Murphy's scarred and gnarled knuckles did land a glancing blow that split the skin over Cody's left eye.

Big Joe swore, his arms flailing the air like the slats on a windmill, as his momentum carried him off balance.

Blood flowed from the cut above Cody's eye and he could taste the bitter bile in the back of his throat as he battled to stand. He spread his legs, planting his feet wide as he stood ready to face the cutthroat. He knew the other revolver remained tucked in his sash, as surely as he knew Murphy meant to beat him to a bloody heap.

Big Joe picked himself up and whirled on Cody, his murderous gray eyes afire with hatred and his face flushed.

"Ya oughta be more careful when ya go tryin' to bring a man in, Pony rider," he growled like a maddened dog.

With his eyes still riveted on Cody, Murphy leaned to his right, bending his knee as he reached for the top of his boot.

"Yeah, I'm tired of funnin' with ya, boy. Can't say I ain't enjoyed battin' ya around, but I got me a purty little woman to get after." The bandit drew the boot gun, leveling it at Cody as he straightened.

Cody's left hand darted like a striking snake to the Colt's handle and plucked it from his sash. The sunlight breaking over the low, rolling hills to the east glinted off the polished steel of the gun barrel.

In that split second Big Joe Murphy saw his mistake.

Cody didn't hesitate a moment. As the revolver cleared his sash he thumbed back the hammer, turned the muzzle on the outlaw, and pulled the trigger.

The bullet plowed into Murphy's belly, doubling him over. He didn't even try to lift his own gun for a shot at Cody. The pistol slipped from his fingers as he pressed both hands into his stomach. He sagged to his knees, then pitched forward into the dust.

Cody emitted a heavy sigh as he lowered the smoking gun to his side. After Big Joe's crushing blow to his ribs, he'd known that he would have to defend himself with his gun. The outlaw had just made it easier. He took a few moments to catch his breath, then quickly searched the area for his other revolver, coming up with it in the dust near Murphy's roan. He laid both guns on the ground and untied the brightly colored material that encircled his waist, wetting one end of it with a small amount of water from his canteen. He dabbed the cut over his eye, then wiped the dust from the rest of his face.

He surveyed the prairie as he wrapped the sash around himself. A slight movement along the northern horizon caught his eye and he froze. The slightest of moves on these vast plains drew immediate attention from a careful eye. And Cody had developed one during his years traversing this wide land. He peered through the growing light for another sign of movement and suddenly he saw it. The sight he beheld caused his heart to leap into his throat. He had spotted a small party of Indians. He couldn't make out their number, or their tribe, but that didn't really matter. Certainly they had heard his gunshot; yet, from this distance, they appeared uninterested. Their presence meant trouble, for they were on a course parallel to the one Murphy had indicated Jenny had taken.

A person unfamiliar with traveling in the wilderness could become disoriented very easily and end up wandering in circles. If that had happened to Jenny, these Indians were bound to pick up her sign. As soon as they disappeared from view, Cody retrieved his pistols, hurriedly reloaded them, then gathered up his hat and made for Champion. He leapt onto the mustang's back and spurred him down the embankment.

A hawk glided through the sky over the spot where Murphy lay, and the tall roan stared after the galloping mustang. A sigh sounded behind the horse and it turned its head. Murphy groaned as he rolled onto his back. For several minutes he didn't move, his eyes staring vacantly at the sky. Finally he pushed himself up into a sitting position. His chin fell upon his heaving chest while he reached inside his bloody shirt. He withdrew the mangled talisman, probing the indentation in its middle. It had intercepted the bullet, saving his life. Big Joe opened his shirt and saw the dark, ugly bruise spreading at the base of his breastbone.

"Fool kid," he muttered as he gingerly touched the contusion. Then he clasped the medal in both hands. "Looks like my luck ain't run out yet."

# CHAPTER 25

MURPHY had been right about one thing: Jenny's horse had cut up the sod, leaving a trail a bat could follow. Cody leaned over the saddle horn, eyeing the tracks as Champion trotted easily across the level. The trail led westward and Cody felt the warm sun on his shoulders as it peaked over the horizon behind him.

The path held to its westerly course for nearly two hours and Cody took that as a good sign. It meant Jenny had used the setting sun as a beacon to keep her headed in the right direction and that made his job easier. However, moments later, the hoofprints disappeared. Cody reined Champion to a halt and swung out of his saddle. He began darting back and forth, inspecting the earth like a hound sniffing for a scent. Suddenly he came upon a small depression where the grass had been beaten down. After careful study he realized he had discovered Jenny's camp. She hadn't continued riding, exhausting her horse as Murphy had speculated she would. Her stopping showed good sense and, once again, proved to Cody she had courage. She had risked Murphy overtaking her to give her horse a much needed rest. The trail she had left provided all of the evidence needed to see she had ridden the animal hard.

Cody crisscrossed the meager camp, searching for a sign of her departure. It didn't take him long to locate it and what he found distressed him. She had headed north not more than an hour ago, perhaps gambling she could find the river, not knowing she risked crossing paths with the Indians he had seen this morning. The only encouraging sign he had seen was that she hadn't started out running her horse. He climbed back aboard the mustang, grasping the reins and wheeling the pony northward.

Champion charged over the prairie like a shooting star streaking across the sky. With his ears back and nostrils flaring, his hooves pounded the earth as they churned up the sod. Upon the pony's back, Cody stretched over the saddle horn, his face so close to the horse's neck that Champion's mane buffeted his cheeks.

Cody halted the mustang as they crested a knoll overlooking a wide plain. In the distance Cody spied a horse and rider. There was no way of knowing for certain that it was Jenny, but Cody didn't doubt for a moment that he had found her. He scanned the rest of the desert as Champion's ribs swelled and contracted rhythmically between his legs. He saw no sign of the Indians, but knew the land's levelness was deceptive. Concealed in its vast sea of grass lay hills behind which several men might hide, or treacherous arroyos that opened suddenly to swallow a galloping horse. However, the path between him and Jenny appeared clear and it wouldn't take long for Champion to close the gap.

"Yo, Champ!" he called, touching his spurs to the mustang's sinewy flanks.

The pony lunged down the hillside and out onto the plain, his hoofs flailing the grass.

Cody felt his heart pounding with anticipation in his chest. Jenny had survived. The strength she possessed had shown itself stronger than what Cody had seen during their ride to Freemont Springs. Alone with Murphy and his cutthroats she hadn't given up. Out here in this wild land she hadn't given up. Cody had heard of men, hardy, robust men, who simply abandoned hope when they found themselves totally isolated in an unforgiving wilderness, or alone among savages, often ending their own lives if they had the chance. Perhaps everyone had a point beyond which they couldn't survive, or chose not to fight any longer. But as Champion roared onto the level plain, Cody was relieved that Jenny had continued her struggle.

Hardly half of another hour had passed when Cody was rewarded with a clear look at Jenny. He desperately yearned to call out to her, but didn't dare without knowing the whereabouts of the Indians he had sighted earlier. He gave the mustang a quick rap with his quirt and Champion sprinted ahead. Suddenly Jenny's face turned toward him. He rose in the saddle as he swept his hat off and waved it in an arc over his head.

Jenny wheeled her horse about, then drove her heels into its sides. The animal sprang into a gallop, bearing down on Cody. As Jenny neared Cody he reined Champion to a skidding halt, raising a roiling cloud of dust. He had leapt from the saddle by the time Jenny pulled up in front of Champion.

"Oh, Cody!" she cried. She jumped from the saddle, tears coursing down her cheeks and cutting through layers of dust. She threw her arms around his neck and pressed her lips to his, then hugged him tightly. "I was so afraid I'd never see you again. So afraid I'd never see anyone again."

His arms encircled her waist and he gently patted her back.

"It's gonna be all right," he said, wishing he didn't have to tell her about the Indians he had seen. He pulled himself free and took hold of her shoulders, staring into her eyes. "But we're not out of trouble yet. We've got to keep movin'."

"Murphy?" Her eyes widened in fear.

"No, not Murphy. He's dead. But I saw some Indians this morning and they were headed in this direction. I haven't seen 'em since, but we best not take any chances."

Jenny nodded.

"We'll need to take it slow for a little while. That'll give Champ some time to rest. I've been pushin' him hard."

Cody helped Jenny back onto her horse, then hoisted himself onto the mustang's back.

"I want to thank you, Cody," she said as they started their horses walking. "For coming after me, that is."

"Nothin' else I could do," he said, staring straight ahead. Then he turned his eyes on her. "I wasn't about to let you go without a fight."

Shortly after midday they stopped at a narrow creek to water the horses and take a rest. Cody and Jenny shared beef jerky and hardtack from his saddlebags and sips of water from Cody's canteen.

"Did Murphy treat you pretty bad?" he inquired, curious, but not wanting to ask any questions that might embarrass her.

"It wasn't as bad as it could've been, I suppose. There was some kind of trouble between Murphy and his men. And they wouldn't let him harm me because they wanted me to care for one of the men who was wounded. But after everyone went in different directions I was afraid of what that meant for me. So, as soon as I got the chance, I ran."

"You did good."

She smiled. "I was scared."

Jenny folded her hands in her lap and stared at them, then at the torn and filthy dress spread in disarray about her.

"I must look awful," she said, attempting to brush the dust from her dress. "I think I'm going to at least wash my face."

She stood and swished past Cody, headed for the creek bank. She knelt there, scooping handfuls of cool water to her face, gently bathing away the dust of the last few days. Suddenly she heard a horse blow on the other side of the creek and her head shot up. She saw an Indian sitting astride his horse, gazing at her, his features hard and cold as though carved in stone.

"Cody." Her call was hardly more than a whisper at first. Then she found her voice and cried out. "Cody!"

He had seen the Indian only moments before her. And he had seen the red man wasn't alone. Three others trailed behind him, herding several ragged-looking ponies toward the creek.

"Come to me, Jenny. But move real slow."

She did as he instructed, backing from the water's edge, her eyes riveted on the Indian. Cody nodded at the brave atop his pony and lifted his hand for a brief wave. The brave didn't move. The others reached the creek, bedecked in little more than loincloths and a solitary feather hanging from a strip of rawhide tied in the hair at the crown of their heads. None carried any firearms, only the primitive weapons they had used for centuries.

"What are we going to do?" Jenny asked as she came to stand beside Cody.

"Stay calm. They want to water their horses and we're done waterin' ours. So we'll just get ready to move on."

The Indians spoke rapidly to one another, without casting so much as a glance at the two whites, but intently studying the two horses standing on the bank.

Cody stooped to retrieve his saddlebags and handed them to Jenny.

"Hang on to these. I'll get the horses."

As Cody started toward their mounts, one of the braves, a small, but hard-bodied man, rode across the creek and onto the bank between the Pony rider and the horses.

"Name!" he demanded, pointing the tip of his lance at Cody.

"Cody Bailey."

His response brought a chorus of chattering from the rest of the men straddling their spent ponies.

The red man who had crossed the creek swung his left leg over his horse's neck and slid to the ground. He stalked toward Cody, his back straight, his chin high. He solemnly placed his palm upon his bronze chest.

"I am Cheyenne," he said with obvious pride. "I am called Pawnee Killer. You are Co-dee?"

Cody furrowed his brow. This Indian seemed to recognize his name.

"Yep. Like I said before, I'm Cody."

"Friend to Standing Bear of the Lakota?"

Cody smiled. "Yes. I know Standing Bear and Red Eagle."

"We," he said, lifting his hand to his comrades, "let you travel our land in peace this day because of Standing Bear."

"Thank you. I won't forget this," Cody said, trying not to show the relief he felt.

The brave turned away and hopped onto the back of his pony. He glared down at Cody.

"Today you travel in peace."

He turned the pony with a hard jerk on the reins and rejoined his companions. From that point they appeared to ignore Cody and Jenny completely.

Cody retrieved the horses, and Jenny and he mounted up and started north. They let the animals walk, as Cody no longer saw any reason for them to hurry. He had enough food to see them through for at least three days if they ate sparingly; besides, he expected to reach one of the ranches along the river long before food became any kind of problem.

That evening the pair camped in the midst of an arid plain. They unsaddled the horses, then began searching for the dried buffalo dung that littered the prairie to use as fuel for their campfire. As darkness descended they prepared the beds, laying their blankets near the fire.

Cody crawled into his covers. He was tired to the soles of his feet. Except for his brief stay in Standing Bear's camp he hadn't had much rest, but now he felt he could sleep without apprehension. He had no doubt he could now see Jenny safely out of the desert and, if she desired, on to Denver. His eyes closed and he slipped into a deep sleep.

Black clouds bubbled over the western horizon well after midnight, obscuring the moon and stars and casting a deep shadow over the land.

Champion's head came up abruptly as his ears twitched one way, then the other. He pawed the dust nervously, emitting a restless nicker. Neither Cody nor Jenny heard him.

"Cody!"

The cry roused him like a slap in the face. He bounded to his feet, drawing one of the Colts as he rose. In the darkness he saw two shadows grappling with one another. He recognized right away that one of them was Jenny, and the other—

"Murphy!"

The pilot tried to pull Jenny in front of him and use her for a shield, but she fought, clawing and scratching like a cornered cat. That gave Cody his chance. He leveled his pistol at Murphy's head and, without hesitation, pulled the trigger.

The outlaw's hands seized his face, releasing Jenny, who tumbled to the ground. Murphy stumbled backward. He tangled his feet and plummeted into the dirt.

Still clutching the smoking revolver, Cody raced to Jenny's side. He knelt on one knee beside her, his left shoulder to Murphy, and started to gather her into his arms. Suddenly Big Joe rolled onto his side, facing them, blood covering his face and dripping from his chin. He clutched the heavy Colt in his hand, aiming it squarely at the Pony rider.

Cody shoved Jenny to the ground as he twisted to bring the pistol in his right hand to bear on the bandit. The big Colt roared and the ball whizzed past Cody's ear. Bailey fired twice, his gun aimed into Murphy's face. The outlaw's visage was shattered by the howling lead that slammed him into the dust, his arms spread wide.

Cody stood, his gun still in his hand, and walked to where Murphy lay. He squatted beside the bandit, studying the wounds he had inflicted upon him. He wanted to make sure the outlaw was really dead. Twice, now, he had been sure he had killed Murphy, only to face him again. This time, however, he had no doubts.

He started to stand, but then caught sight of the medallion that lay against the base of Murphy's throat. It appeared to be a gold disk on a rawhide string. He turned it over in his hand, looking for some kind of inscription, but didn't find anything. He gave it a hard jerk, popping it free of the rawhide. If it was solid gold Jenny could use the money it would bring.

He returned to Jenny's side and took her into his arms.

"Are you all right?"

She threw her arms around him as tears flooded her eyes.

"Jenny?"

She choked back a sob and sniffed hard.

"I'm all right." She sniffed again. "I guess I just lost control of myself."

"I'd say you were entitled."

He embraced her, rocking her gently in his arms, until she regained her composure. Then he stood and left her side, walking over to where Big Joe laid spread-eagled in the dust, his face blown away and unrecognizable. Jenny walked up beside him.

"Are you going to bury him?"

"What do you think?"

She grasped his arm and looked into his eyes.

"I think there's time."

In the late afternoon of the following day they inter-cepted a small posse led by John Butler. Two days later they reached Parker's Junction and Silas Bonner's Pony station, where Cody's job still waited.

If you have enjoyed this book and would like to receive details on other Walker Western titles, please write to:

Western Editor
Walker and Company
720 Fifth Avenue
New York, NY 10019